CULLY
AND THE TYRANT

ORRIS SLADE

Contents

Prologue

Durango, Colorado

Samuel "Cully" McCullough weaved through the bustling crowd that had collected at Durango's rodeo and cattle auction event. Laughter, excitement, and music echoed through the streets. His nose crinkled at the smell of manure and sweet confections that mingled in the air.

The games, contests, and other activities brought the community together in a way that had never failed to return that glimmer of hope in Cully's gaze. Bull riding, chuck wagon races, bareback bronco riding, steer wrestling, and more of the typical rodeo events took place all around him.

A few the local youths were busy playing horseshoes to his left as he strolled. The corners of his mouth twitched in a phantom smile at a sticky toddler covered in what may have been a slice of pie at one point. Cully knelt down by the small girl and retied the bow in her hair when he noticed it had come undone.

When the bow was neat and tidy, the sweet girl hid in the crook of her mother's neck and shied away. He chuckled and greeted the woman with a simple nod. "Ma'am."

"Thank you, I hadn't noticed." She offered her free hand while the other cradled her daughter. "You must be Cully."

"Guilty as charged, Missus—"

"Miss," she corrected. "Abigail Mills."

Cully grasped the woman's hand and shook it gently. He kept his smile firmly in place so that she was not overwhelmed by the sheer size of him. People were often surprised by his height, but he couldn't do much about that. "Samuel McCullough," he said.

"Pleasure to meet you."

Cully continued down the road not much longer after that. Anyone that recognized him stared briefly at his passing, but only those closest to Cully actually approached him. Several of the people he had saved or worked contracts for in the past gave him a tight hug or companionable pat on the back.

Mostly, people stared at him as though they were awestruck by his presence. Cully didn't know what to make of that. It was no secret that he usually showed up at these events alone—his bachelor status a well-known fact, which was much to the delight of the young ladies in town.

A few ladies wiggled their fingers in his direction with bright smiles that decorated their faces. Giggles and flirty winks came flying at him from so many directions, it caused Cully's head to spin. The young lady with copper curls and light freckles on her cheeks was brave enough to blow him a little kiss.

To which Cully responded by ducking his head as his cheeks blushed bashfully. "Enjoy your day, ladies." Something about their behavior reminded him of pretty birds basking in warm sunlight. All flutter and fussing.

He eventually made his way over to a table where Wesley Philbrook and his lovely wife, Grace, waited for him. His old friend Caden Warren had brought along Mary and the new baby for the excitement and experience. Heck, even Charlotte Dean and Wolf came out of hiding long enough to do some mingling.

Cully couldn't help the warmth that spread through his chest at the sight of their happiness. The only problem was Cully was the only person there without a significant other. He didn't have a wife to pull close and whisper to or someone to share his burden with.

Instead of dwelling on the thought, he tried his best to ignore the pang of jealousy that twisted in his gut. Fate had denied him a family of his own thus far, but he had faith that he would find it, eventually. Cully wanted to ask Wesley if he had heard from Mateo since he had set out to find his sister, Maria, but decided it wasn't any of his business. If Mateo wanted him to know, he would speak to Cully directly.

The Rodriguez siblings were strong. Whatever trouble they had gotten themselves into, they could handle it.

Cully reached over and lifted Caden's baby girl into his arms and cradled the tiny infant's head in the palm of his large hand. "It's a good thing you look like your mama, little girl. Or else we'd be worried about findin' you a suitor if you had your daddy's ugly mug," Cully drawled sarcastically.

Caden cut him a dirty look before placing a kiss on Mary's cheek. "The ladies tend to find me especially handsome. That's how I got my beautiful wife. Ain't that right, sweetheart?"

Mary rolled her eyes at her husband and smiled at Cully.

Wolf barked out a rush of laughter that was cut off by Charlotte hitting him in arm. "What? He clearly never recovered from his past injuries if he believes anyone other than Mary could find him handsome."

As the playful banter continued, Cully rocked the precious child in his arms. Suddenly he felt someone hug his shoulders from behind. Looking up, he held the gaze of Betty Hamish. Arthur stood beside his wife with pride shining in his eyes.

"I know that last job was hard for you, son. But I want you to know that your father would have been proud. Benjamin was a good man and I'm happy to see that you've grown to be a fine one yourself." Arthur could not have known how much his words meant to Cully.

"Everyone has to suffer a loss in their career at least once. I'm just glad mine ended with the desired result."

Arthur patted him on the arm and said, "The Lord has good things planned for you, Cully. Remember that."

Betty sat beside Cully and fussed over the cooing child in his arms. Caden chatted with Arthur and the rest of the group chatted amicably amongst each other. He often wondered how his parents would think of this life. Would they approve? Or would he have been cast out of the church and the community for the violence that seemed to follow him?

No, somewhere in his mind, he knew he did God's work.

Or at least gave him a helping hand.

Someone had to keep the peace in the corrupt lands of the west and bring the bad guys to justice. Cully knew he wasn't exactly hero material, but he liked to think he made a difference. He may not have everything he wanted, but he was on his way to having everything he needed.

After the baby started fussing, Cully handed her back to her mother while he and his friends went to watch the races. The first half was uneventful and a little underwhelming. The second half of the race was when things got interesting enough to convince Cully to stay in his seat. It was a good show. But toward the end there was speculation on who would be the four finalists.

Cully grabbed what was left of his bag of peanuts and headed down to the corral to pay a visit to one of his old friends, Art Meachan. He and Art went way back, and Cully had a sense of respect for the man.

As he approached the area, Cully heard shouting. He slowed his pace and eased toward the stable, careful to stay out of sight while he observed the situation before him. No need to rush into something before he knew what it was about.

"I ain't askin' you to do much, Art! I'm only suggestin' that you have a little accident that throws the race," someone offered. Cully recognized the voice of Ed Bissel trying to bribe his friend. "So far, you're the first-place contender and folks are bettin' on you. Why don't you fall off your horse or somethin', lose the race, and then all four of us can divide up the prizes and take home a bit of a profit?"

"Are you hearin' yourself, Ed?" Art yelled. "Ain't no way I'm riskin' my reputation and my dignity for y'all."

The argument grew heated. However, no altercation had occurred yet, so Cully didn't see the need to intervene. Just when he had decided to stay out of the situation entirely, he noticed that Art was outnumbered and Ed had picked up a shovel. Ed moved up behind Art to hit him when Cully pushed his way through the stable. He knocked Ed over as he was raising up the shovel.

So much for not getting involved...

Cully feels a sharp sting after the handle of a broom was broken over his back. He turned around and landed a hefty punch on one of the men who had tried to bribe Art. Back to back, Art and Cully brawled against the other men left standing. For a moment, Cully thought his friend had gone a bit mad when he realized Art had been laughing the entire time.

They quickly subdued them. Art returned to his preparations for the final portion of the race. Cully went to alert the event coordinators of what had happened. Ed Bissel was disqualified from continuing in the race. The other contenders got to keep their positions but were threatened with disciplinary actions if they were caught fighting again.

Satisfied with another job well done, Cully returned to his seat. He was a bit disappointed that he had lost his bag of peanuts in the scuffle, but he was soon placated after Grace handed him a tiny square of fudge from a tin container in her hands. Cully accepted the sweet delight even if he wasn't one for sweets to begin with. It had been Grace's smile that made sure he wasn't able to deny her offer.

Cully popped the treat in his mouth and reached for the baby once again. He was momentarily distracted from the race when he noticed a few women around his age releasing a blissful sigh at the sight of a domesticated man. Cully couldn't help but chuckle to himself. The tiny creature in his arms had his finger in a tight grip as she slowly dozed off.

He nearly missed the look of longing in Charlotte's expression, but he winked at her to let her know that he understood how she felt. Wolf and Charlotte revealed in one of their letters that they were having trouble conceiving a child. Cully wished them the best of luck but made sure to remind them that there were plenty of orphaned children in need of a good home.

Cully looked up as Mary laughed openly when she noticed him scowling at some patrons sitting around them. He looked like he was tempted to pull out his gun if they woke the baby. His cheeks brightened a bit as his expression softened under her gaze. She wiped tears of joy from her eyes and smiled at him.

Before he could reply, the race came to an end without any more problems. Art came in second place, which was impressive to say the least, given the number of racers that had been involved in the event, so Cully invited him down to the saloon to celebrate.

Caden and Mary decided to return to the hotel so they could turn in for the night. Cully was reluctant to hand over the sleeping child. Caden gave him a strange look and said, "You'll be one heck of a father one of these days, Cully."

Wolf, Charlotte, Grace, Wesley, Art, and Cully moseyed on down to the saloon for some good beer and bad food. They shared stories, most of which involved Cully saving somebody's hide. He scoffed, rolled his eyes, and sipped his beer. By the time the night wound down, the corners of Cully's eyes were crinkled and his cheeks hurt from laughing too much. He needed days of happiness to get him through the rest of the year.

Cully said goodbye to his friends and packed up his things before he returned to Samson. He patted his horse affectionately and saddled up for the ride home.

Chapter 1

Bakewell Ranch

Five miles outside of Durango, Colorado

Billy Voss sat down in a leather wingback chair beside the crackling fire. He watched with a scowl on his face as the flames danced. Billy was a man known for getting what he wanted, no matter the cost to anybody else. A past as mysterious as the man who had lived it, no one knew exactly where he came from or who he was. Billy Voss was a man without a reputation.

That was soon to change.

The only thing that matched his ambition was his greed. And his newly purchased ranch home and the speck of land just wasn't enough, it seemed. Billy had money—coins weren't what he yearned for. Land in the west was worth far more than the government's dollars.

Land was power. And he wanted the resources, the homesteads, and the benefits that came with owning land. His father always used to say, "Own the land and you own the people." And those words had not wronged him since he left his family home back east. He looked around at the empty space of the old Bakewell Ranch he had swindled.

Billy had hired some local carpenters to gut the entire place of everything that hadn't been a necessity. Now the walls went up to the beams that supported the roof. No staircases, no second story, and no attic. The only room that remained was a kitchen... and the cellar beneath the house.

Everything had been opened to allow the air to flow naturally. Sunlight came in through the windows oddly placed at irregular intervals. Billy hated feeling boxed in or restricted in any way. All he needed was his tumbler of whiskey, his favorite chair, and a nice fire to feel relaxed.

Anything else was just a waste of his time.

Physical objects were just a pretty way people liked to pretend they weren't as barbaric as humanity had always been. People didn't change, the rest of the world did. He learned that much when he had fought in the war. Buildings came down just as fast as they were put up.

Forests disappeared, volcanoes erupted, mountains grew taller, the ocean got wider, but people never changed. They all like to pretend that acting civilized meant their basic animal instincts no longer existed. Billy scoffed at the thought. He'd seen more so-called civilized folk pull a trigger faster than a bandit with a lawman on his trail.

Billy looked down at the crinkled map he held balled up in his fist. The only fresh water source for miles was on Denis Seeley's property, and Billy fully intended to gain ownership of that property. It would be just another investment toward his goal to gain control over the area.

He could send his men do a little poking around to see what made the man tick, but Billy wanted to make an offer in person. Every man had a price, and he was willing to bet that the people of Durango, Colorado didn't hold their standards too high. Not with all the failed attempts to build successful ranches and farms. Folks around these parts were desperate.

———————

Denis Seeley was a charitable man. He had just used his last bit of extra money to send a train ticket to Georgia so his granddaughter Alice could come stay with him. She mentioned something about hitting a rough patch with her fiancé, but Denis had cut off her explanation and insisted she move.

After losing his wife and his old friend, Reverend Benjamin McCullough, Denis felt like home had taken on a new meaning over the years. He still attended church every Sunday, and he took care of his home, but he had to cut back on his own money in order to keep paying the ranch hands a fair wage. Denis would rather go hungry than watch someone else scrape together pennies just to eat. No, he took care of those who were loyal to him, even if it meant he was just barely getting by himself.

He grumbled under his breath as he walked into the kitchen to pour himself a cup of Arbuckles' Ariosa coffee, his favorite. The beans had been a gift from one of the ladies at the church who was sweet on him. His fingers absentmindedly stroked his wedding band.

A knock sounded at the front door. Denis didn't get many visitors unless something was arranged ahead of time, so he couldn't imagine who would be knocking at his door first thing on a Sunday morning.

"Can I help you?" he asked.

Something foul churned in his stomach the instant the stranger turned around. The man wore a navy-blue suit beneath a camel trench coat. He removed his hat as his lips curled into a smile that had Denis peeking at the ground to see if he could find a trail of slime leading to his door.

"Hello. My name is Billy Voss. It's a pleasure to see the man behind the name, Mr. Seeley," the man said.

Each word he spoke had been clipped and polished. Billy Voss definitely wasn't a local. Although he dressed like a man from New York, Denis heard the subtle accent hidden beneath his façade that was reminiscent of the northern Midwest territories. Even so, he grasped Billy Voss's outstretched hand in a firm grip and gave it a little shake.

With hair as black and slick as an oil spill, Billy peered over Denis's shoulder with his unsettling blue eyes. "It's a bit cold out here," he said blatantly.

Denis hesitated just slightly before he allowed the man entrance in his home. "Would you like a cup of coffee?"

"Yes, thank you kindly."

He led Billy Voss into his kitchen and poured a second cup before offering it to the man. Denis waited with a suspicious feeling clawing away at his spine. "Is this just a friendly introduction and a brief chat or did you have somethin' else in mind?" Denis questioned.

"Just getting to know my neighbors."

"So you're the one who bought the old Bakewell place," he muttered before taking a sip of his coffee.

"Indeed, I am," Billy confirmed. "I can see you are a smart man, Mr. Seeley. So I will not insult your intelligence any further. As much as I wish this visit were just a small chat between neighbors, my true intentions are to make you an offer for your property."

Denis snorted. He sort of respected the man's outspokenness. "My property, huh? I don't know where exactly you come from, boy. But there ain't no need to color what you're sayin' with uppity words around here. And I ain't interested in sellin' my ranch."

"You have not even heard my offer."

"Don't need to," Denis stated simply. "Ain't enough money in the world that could get me to hand over my land."

Billy Voss's face was red and twisted with frustration, but only for a brief moment until that icy mask of indifference slid back into place. "Excuse my candor, Mr. Seeley. But I can smell the poverty on your skin. The ranch looks lovely and flourishing from the outside looking in—I'm sure you have the people of this pathetic town fooled by your antics, but you and I know the truth about your financial status."

Denis stared in shock at both Billy's words and how he scowled down at his cup as though the coffee had personally offended his taste buds. Sometimes, Denis didn't like comprehending that his first impressions of people were true, especially when they weren't very good. "Get out."

"At least let me show you the numbers," Billy said before Denis could tell him to go dance with the devil.

His heart nearly seized up after he had taken in the number of zeros attached to the ridiculous offer on his ranch. "My ranch ain't worth this kind of cash. Only a crazy person would offer somethin' like this."

"Money is not an issue. I want this land, and I will have it."

"I don't think I like your tone, Mister." Tension clung to the air and made Denis wish he had kept the ranch hands around a little longer, but it was Sunday. And he always gave the boys Sunday off in hopes he would run into them at the church.

"Take the papers, read them over, and I'll be back in a few days. Although, if you feel inclined to ignore my offer, I might just have to motivate you—"

"Enough. Get out of my house."

Billy Voss set down his coffee cup and fussed with his jacked a lot longer than necessary. The smile on his face never faltered.

Denis scowled at him and lifted his arm to point at the front door. "You can see yourself out, seein' as it'll be the last time you ever see the inside of this house."

"Don't be too sure about that, Mr. Seeley. You will sell me your property or... Let's just say, I don't take rejection well."

When Billy Voss finally left, Denis locked the door and carried his old bones up the stairs to his bedroom. He cleaned up, shaved, and got dressed for church. In his mind, Denis knew that the Lord would see him through his struggles. The only thing he had to do was to keep the faith in his heart burning and an endless amount of patience in his soul.

After years of dealing with entitled people trying to take his home from him, Denis was sure that, like the rest, Billy Voss wouldn't be too much of a bother. Sure, the ranch wasn't in the best shape financially, but the hands were happy, there was food on the table each night, and a small profit helped keep things going. He had a small, but blessed life.

———————

His time at the church the following Sunday had done wonders to ease his stresses. But the unmistakable sight of his homestead on fire quickly stifled his relief. The smoke in the air caused Denis to cough roughly into his handkerchief. The first thought that entered his mind was that he and Alice didn't have a home anymore. And the hands were out of jobs.

It was Billy Voss. It had to be. There was no one else in Colorado that he had any issues with. Although it had been staged as a random bandit attack or a run-of-the-mill cattle raid, there was something darker beneath the surface. The horses and cattle were scattered across the territory, most likely picked off by wild animals or salvaged by the other nearby ranches. Without livestock, there wasn't much hope of rebuilding or starting up again.

Denis sighed heavily and brushed the tears from his eyes. There was only one man he knew that could fix this injustice. Benjamin McCullough's son lived around these parts. He often accepted contracts, solved problems, and helped common folk stay decent and honest even when the world seemed to work against them. Cully was Denis's last and only hope to save his homestead.

He stayed with his hired hands and helped put out the fire. By the time the flames were quenched, there wasn't much left but an empty shell of his home. Blackened and damaged, the foundation still seemed sturdy, but the rest would need to be demolished. Denis fought to find the silver lining.

He didn't have much money left, but he prayed with all of his heart that it was enough to convince Samuel McCullough to help him rebuild his family home. Even if he was unable to get the ranch back up and operational by the time Alice arrived, he just needed a place she could one day inherit.

That was all that really mattered.

Chapter 2

Cully sat astride Samson as he eased onto Denis Seeley's property. He had received a letter from his father's old friend with the words of a desperate man dripping from each page. The situation Denis had described in his letter made Cully sick to his stomach. Although the man had yet to mention anyone he suspected was behind the attack, Cully could sense the slight accusatory undertone.

The charred remains of a barn and a farmhouse were the only structures on the land. A nice freshwater stream flowed along the edges of the property. Cully frowned in confusion. There were only four functioning ranches within a five-mile radius. If the situation wasn't personal to Denis, then whoever set his home ablaze could be targeting the other settlements.

Cully dismounted and tied Samson before he approached the barn. A group of neighbors had banded together to help rebuild it. There was a strong sense of family and community in the area, which Cully was proud to be a part of. He smiled at everyone and tipped his hat in greeting, making sure he took the time to introduce himself to the people he was less acquainted with.

His gaze scanned the area for Denis, but he couldn't spot him right away. A young lady approached him with an air of timidity about her. She was modest and very traditional if her behavior and clothing was anything to go by. It was most likely that she had been raised in a conservative Christian home.

"Can I help you, sir?" she asked in a soft-spoken voice.

"My name is Samuel McCullough, ma'am. I'm here to see Denis Seeley. He sent me a letter a while back."

The young lady wiped her hands off on her apron and reached out to shake his hand. Cully resisted the urge to tell her that she had a smear of soot on her right cheek and accepted her hand. She reminded Cully of his sister, Doris.

"My name is Alice Seeley. It's a pleasure to see you again, Mr. McCullough," she said delicately. He couldn't believe his eyes. Little Alice Seeley was all grown up. And from the looks of it, she had moved back to town. "My grandfather is watering the horses we were able to round up."

Cully nodded his thanks and headed for the stream, reminiscing about the times they had sat beside one another at his father's church.

Denis Seeley was indeed tending to his horses when he walked over. There was a slight moment of recognition before sadness entered the man's eyes. "You look so much like him..."

Cully shifted uncomfortably on his feet and glanced down at his muddied boots. Denis walked over and put his arms around him, and for a moment he felt like he was a kid again. The sadness he had buried down deep after losing his parents came rushing to the surface as he returned the man's embrace.

It was hard to remember sometimes that he hadn't been the only one to lose people that day. When the gang rode into his hometown, he had been no more than a boy—unable to defend himself or his family. That was nearly ten years ago, but the pain was still raw and it cut Cully down to his soul.

And on top of everything else that had happened to him, he felt the guilt of leaving behind his sister. Cully had only been sixteen years old when he and Doris had been orphaned. But his mind had been on his mission and leaving her in the care of others when he left town two years later was what had been the best option at the time.

When the intense reunion came back down to a light simmer, Cully and Denis separated. "I ran into that granddaughter of yours. She was... about eleven years old when I last saw her. How is Sally Mae doin' these days, sir?"

"My daughter is doin' just fine. She and her husband came up to visit last winter. Alice will be stayin' here for good now." Denis beamed. "Family is what life is all about. Well, that and servin' the good Lord. You seen your sister lately?"

Cully swallowed his shame. It didn't feel right telling a man like Denis Seeley that he hadn't had much time for family over the past several months. They kept in touch through letters and the occasional visit whenever he came to town, but he hated wondering what his precious Doris thought about his reputation. She had always been a sweet girl with a passive heart and some things Cully was forced to do in the name of justice would go against her strong beliefs. "We talk when we can," he replied weakly.

Denis didn't pry, he got right down to business. "It's that no good Billy Voss, I'm tellin' you. Should have heard the way he threatened me. And the look in his eyes—man, he was somethin' else. Wouldn't take no for an answer after he tried to buy the ranch out from under me."

Suspicion wasn't proof. And before Cully could confront someone for the crime, there had to be proof that one had even taken place to begin with. Arson was hard to prove, extortion even more so. "Any witnesses that heard him threaten you?"

"No. Just me and him, sittin' in the kitchen."

"What about threatenin' letters or intimidation tactics?" Cully didn't like where this was headed already.

"Just the ridiculous offer he made for the land."

"Denis, listen." Cully sighed, "You ain't givin' me much to work with. There doesn't seem to be much evidence besides the fire itself. Is it possible you forgot the coffee pot on the stove or the fireplace was still burnin' when you went to church?"

"I might be older, son. But I ain't out of my mind with age yet. I know for a fact that I didn't leave anythin' burnin'."

"Well, until I can find some evidence, I'll camp out on the property to keep an eye on the place. Maybe I'll pitch in and help out with rebuildin' the place, too. I ain't gonna leave until we know for sure. You have my word."

Denis gave him a sad smile and patted his shoulder before turning back to his horses. Cully walked back to the barn and took the saddle off Samson. When his horse was comfortable, he marched him over to the temporary, makeshift corral the community had put together to keep the horses on the property while they rebuilt the barn and stables.

He adjusted his shirt and fastened his jacket a bit tighter. Alice smiled up at him kindly when he entered the rough-framed barn that was currently under construction. Cully counted a minimum of sixteen men who were all eager to help Denis and Alice put their lives back together. He smiled back and got to work lifting the beams and picking up a hammer.

It felt good to do something that resembled normalcy. Cully wondered what his life would have been like if that tragic night hadn't happened all those years ago. Would he have been a reverend like his father? Would he have been a lawman? An honest carpenter, perhaps? He wasn't sure exactly.

"Alice?" he called.

She turned to him with even more black smudges on her face.

Cully chuckled and handed her a handkerchief.

Alice accepted it gracefully and attempted to hide her meek blushing behind a confidence that was all steam and no truth. "Yes?"

"Did your grandfather ever talk to you about a man named Billy Voss?" Cully asked.

"No, but most of the people in town say he's looking to buy up homesteads around here. He just moved into the Bakewell Ranch not too far from where you're at."

"I'll be lookin' into a few things involvin' the fire while I'm helpin' out around here. Just thought I'd let you know because you'll probably be seein' a lot of me over the next few days." Cully hammered in a particularly stubborn nail.

Alice continued her current task of holding his ladder steady as she spoke. "I remember you from when I was a little girl. You were always so kind to me, Mr. McCullough."

"That so?"

"Sure is. You always used to look out for me when the other kids were being mean. I'll never forget the day you told me that even shy girls are allowed to be brave."

It sounded like something he would have said to a young girl down on her luck. But he grew concerned at the wistful tone in Alice's voice. "Yeah. If I remember correctly, you followed that up by ramblin' on about how bees were majestic creatures and how they needed to be protected so your mama could make you a honey cake."

Alice blushed again. It was nice to chat with a childhood friend after so many years of being apart. And even though she was no longer the small-town girl he had known in his youth, Cully was happy to see that her move east hadn't dampened her spirit—at least not all of it.

There was still a glimmer of the child she had once been in her eyes. Her voice was barely a whisper as she said, "He's scared. My grandfather is afraid someone will try to hurt me to get the ranch. I tried to tell him that no one here would do such a thing, but then he gets quiet..."

"Denis just wants you to be safe. If anyone tries to harm you or anybody else in Durango, they'll be answerin' to me. Got that? And if they want to start trouble, then I'll be there to bust down their door and haul them off to the sheriff."

She visibly calmed. Something had the Seeley family spooked half out of their minds. Whatever impression this Billy Voss had made, it wasn't good. Still, impressions and suspicions were not enough to put someone behind bars. Cully had hunted down his fair share of cunning men, and if that was what they were dealing with... he was willing to believe that finding proof would be harder than they expected.

He was used to facing long odds, but Denis may just have this all wrong. Cully would do his best, dig up some dirt, and if he didn't find anything he would head on out after the rebuild. Hopefully his presence and added security along with Denis and Alice's faith would be enough to put their minds at ease.

"So what did you do while you were back in Georgia?"

"I got a job working at a new hospital while I went to school. There weren't many jobs for girls like me there that hadn't come from decent money. But I worked hard until I met Lawrence and got engaged."

Cully frowned in thought. "Why ain't he here with you?"

"After he convinced me to leave my job and to give up on school, he got involved in a new business venture. He left for New York, and after six months of waiting to hear from him or see him come home, he finally sent a letter letting me know that he wasn't coming back. He had met someone, and they were married by the time the letter reached me," Alice explained. Her voice was still quiet but tinged with bitterness.

She was still young, and the first heartbreak was always the worst, so Cully didn't fault her for the bitterness. "Men like him don't deserve your anger, Alice. Trust me, he'll be livin' a life of regret before you know it, and you'll move on to the person who is right for you."

Her smile was filled with gratitude. Cully started to pound in the nails on the rafters again as sweat beaded on his forehead. It felt good to work without a rifle in his hand for once.

Chapter 3

Cully walked into the W.B. Hugus Company Store in Durango to make a few purchases. He wandered around, looking at the items available when he noticed the shopkeeper, Jerry, staring. He paid the other man no mind until he was finished shopping. There were some ridiculous things that just seemed like a waste of money, a few gimmicky trinkets nestled among the supplies for visitors, and a few shameless self-promotion business cards.

He walked over and placed some hardtack, a bag of buckwheat flour, some salt pork, a bag of potatoes, a basket of eggs, and a jar of butter on the countertop and asked, "How's business goin' lately, Jerry?"

"Not bad, Cully. How 'bout yourself?"

"I'm in town for a few weeks helpin' out Denis with the restorations and gettin' things up and runnin' again." Cully waited before asking, "You know anythin' in particular about a man named Billy Voss?"

Subtle worry flashed in the man's eyes. "Nope."

"Heard he just moved in to the old Bakewell place. Ain't much of a social guy, from what people are chattin' about. Thought maybe he came by to pick somethin' up, and the two of y'all might have talked."

"Nope."

"All right, then. Take care of the family, and I hope y'all have a good week. Have a nice day, Jerry." *Strange,* Cully thought. Something about Jerry's reaction to Billy Voss's name seemed evasive at the very least.

Cully tucked that bit of information away in the back of his mind for later contemplation, paid for his items, and left the store. He strolled down the street, greeting folks and shaking hands. It was a long and cold walk to the sheriff's office, but Cully wanted some time to stretch his legs. He spent hours and sometimes days in the saddle with Samson or fighting off another outlaw, so these moments of leisure were rare.

Sheriff Lassiter's face was red from the cold as it took on a smile so wide, Cully thought the man might do some permanent damage. Jake Lassiter was a good friend and a good man of the law, so he didn't waste much time getting down to the thick of things. "Ain't got a way to heat this place up, Jake?"

"Dang near burned the place down when I tried. Didn't have time to clean the wood burner out this week, so I've been keepin' warm at the saloon. What can I do for you, Cully?"

"I've been helpin' out Denis Seeley with rebuildin' his home after the fire. I was askin' about what's new around town, and people mentioned a man named Billy Voss who's lookin' to purchase land near here. I ain't never heard of Voss before, but I was hopin' you might fill me in a bit," Cully responded.

Sheriff Lassiter huffed. "Checked on him as soon as he rode into town a few weeks back. Only thing I found on him was an old embezzlement charge up in Chicago a few years ago. Voss was never charged before he left town 'cause there was no evidence to prove there had been a crime. The Pinkertons have been askin' about Voss and his men for questionin' as well."

Cully scratched his chin thoughtfully. "He ain't caused no trouble here? No threats or extortion? I'm not reachin' for a reason to put him away, I just need to know if the people of this fine community are safe."

"Seemed like a normal enough guy if you're fond of leeches. I don't know what kind of business he's runnin', but somethin' about him is just *wrong*. He leaves a foul taste in my mouth every time I see him. But I ain't gonna judge him too harshly until he does somethin' against the law. No one has reported anythin' or really spoken to him. Seems a bit too private for small talk—or any sort of talkin' for that matter. Just comes into town for the necessities and nothin' more." Sheriff Lassiter rocked in his chair a bit, deep in contemplation.

"Does Voss have any reason to use intimidation to get what he wants? There's a lot of good land out here, but fresh water and resources are hard to come by with so much acreage. Seen people do some awful stuff for less."

Billy Voss seemed to be as big of a mystery as the fire. Incidents where Voss was the suspect but no proof could be found. Coincidence? Maybe. There was nothing that connected these suspicions, which meant there isn't a pattern. Most outlaws, crooks, thugs, and swindlers had a unique signature. Or at least they liked a consistency in their operation.

Voss was a businessman if Cully had to guess. Which meant that he couldn't use his normal tactics in finding out whether the man was innocent.

Sheriff Lassiter said, "Voss seemed eager to learn about the major homesteads surroundin' Durango. But he ain't threatened anybody from what I know."

"He got men workin' on the ranch?"

"From what I saw, yeah. Looked heavily armed and professional. Although, they didn't seem like the sort that was needed to run a ranch."

Interesting. It sounded like Billy Voss may have hired a few gunslingers for protection. Cully left after the sheriff indicated with a shake of his head that he had no further information.

No one in town thought the fire was anything malicious, but Denis had been convinced otherwise. It was possible that his father's old friend was just distrustful, but Cully had known Denis and his family longer than he could remember, and they weren't the sort of people to panic under pressure.

The rebuilt church where his father used to preach beckoned him through the doors. It was the location he had told his sister to meet him. He had sent a message to Doris, hoping she would agree to speak with him. Her response had been short and sweet, so Cully was confident she would show up.

He closed the church doors quietly and shook the snow off his jacket, removed his hat, and walked down the center aisle. After adjusting his clothing, he sat in the first pew and looked up at the large wooden cross behind the podium. No one else was in church on a Tuesday afternoon, so it was the best time to clear his thoughts.

Every time Cully came back home, he felt like he was a small boy in a town full of ghosts. His presence merely haunted the streets of Durango, a constant reminder of what people had lost in the attack. The same fear, shame, and sadness washed over him. He felt weakened by it, and he found himself questioning his vow. Was it even worth it anymore?

Cully felt as though he needed to make things better between him and Doris. His efforts over the years had been well received by her. They were close as siblings could be, but they didn't always agree on things. No matter what had happened, they were family, and she was still his little sister. And when she sat down beside him, the gratitude he felt in his heart was overwhelming. "Doris."

"Sam." Doris's voice was hesitant but kind. She was the only person he allowed to call him that as she had done so since they were children. Cully didn't have to turn toward her to be able to hear the slight smile in her words.

"I'm glad you got my letter. Anythin' goin' on with you since we last spoke that I should know about? You don't say much in your replies."

"Well, Ethan and I were glad you could make it to the wedding last year. We're hoping to start a family as soon as he gets a respectable job with decent wages."

"Ethan Hawes has been sweet on you since y'all were old enough to waddle around the house. Always knew you kids would end up together," he recollected. "Ma and Pa would be happy to know that you're doin' fine, Doris. Even more so if they knew you were thinkin' about havin' children."

"They know, Sam. I pray to God every night, and I know that He, along with them, are watching over me. Watching over us."

Silence fell between the siblings. Cully nearly cursed under his breath but quickly reminded himself of where he was sitting. Talking about their parents was always difficult. He reached over and clasped Doris's hand in his own. Her pale, fragile fingers weren't that different from when she had been a child. The small silver ring on her finger made him feel an unwelcome stab of envy.

"What's this all really about, Sam?" she asked finally. "You have me worried."

"I missed you, and I was back in town with some time on my hands, so I thought I would see you, even if it was just briefly. You're my sister, and there are times when I just need someone to have a conversation with that doesn't know me by my reputation. Only you know who I really am."

"It ain't like we're strangers, Sam. You can always come by the farm for another visit. Ethan and I know you're away a lot, but we're happy to have you visit when you can. You still feel guilty for leaving town all those years ago. And I have to admit that I was traumatized, praying my heart out each night for your safety. Every week, I waited to hear from you. Hoping the time never arrived that the letters stopped coming. But you've more than made up for that over the years."

"You were with good people, Doris. They took good care of us, but I had to leave. There were some things that I needed to do back then that I thought no one would understand," Cully explained. "There was no way I could have put you in danger by taking you with me. I had to go on my own."

"You always sent money, taking care of me even if you were off handling some job. I forgave you a long time ago for leaving, but I don't see why you can't let go of the past. The life you live... it's dangerous, Sam."

Cully wanted to remove that look of uncertainty from her features—a face so much like his mother's that it took his breath away. Sometimes Doris looked so much like her that he couldn't stand it, an ache forming in his chest where his heart was supposed to be. "I just need you to understand that what I do is important. You don't have to approve or even support me, but I need you to understand."

"Why are you so certain that this is the path that God has chosen for you, Sam? Did you ever stop to think that you could be something else?" Doris's voice took on a certain twang that sounded suspiciously like his voice. "*My name is Samuel McCullough, but my friends call me Cully. And I'm here to save the day and rid the world of evil.*"

He couldn't help but laugh at her playful, improvised mocking of his well-known introduction. It wasn't perfect, but it sounded as foolish as he felt saying it. Cully missed letting his guard down around people—it often ended badly for him, but with his sister, he knew he was safe to do so. He wrapped his arm around Doris's shoulders and held her close.

The sunlight streamed in through the stained-glass windows of the church as peace fell upon them. "I don't think I'm good enough for a normal life anymore. No matter how much I might want one, I think when it's all said and done, I won't be the same person anymore."

"What has shaken your faith, Sam?"

"When you've seen as much evil as I have, Doris, you start to question things. I've been around a lot of violence and other things I won't trouble you with. But even though I still believe, my faith ain't what it used to be when we were younger. I'm not who I used to be." Cully cleared his throat and tried to force a smile back on his face. "Gonna name your first son after your big brother?"

Doris's soft laughter was worth the effort. "I won't name my son Cully, if that's what you mean. But I like the name Sam. So maybe..." Her smile was a little sad, and her eyes were damp, so Cully pulled her into a comforting hug. Over everything else, his duty was to his family and his job was the protective older brother Doris deserved.

"Don't you cry, Doris Ann McCullough Hawes. Heck, you're the reason I'm stickin' around Durango in the first place. I ain't leavin' you behind no more." Cully slowly rocked his sister as she sobbed against his shoulder. He knew she cried, not for herself, but for him. There wasn't a selfish bone in Doris's body, and Cully loved her even more for it. If heaven was missing an angel, he was holding her in his arms.

Chapter 4

Cully decided to take the bull by the horns and pay Billy Voss a welcoming visit. A few armed men waited at the end of the main road that led to the ranch house. They insisted that he dismount and walk Samson to a corral. He hopped down from the saddle, ignoring how his knees protested the sudden shift in weight, and whistled for Samson to follow.

The two old friends walked side by side as they observed the property. Sheriff Lassiter had been right; the Bakewell Ranch was heavily guarded by at least three or four armed men. None of them seemed to recognize Cully, so he decided to use that little nugget of luck to his advantage.

He kept Samson in a place that was visible from the house, just in case things got a little complicated after the chat between him and Voss. The inside of the house had been more than a surprise. The entire thing had been stripped of its character and turned into nothing more than a roof, a foundation, and a few walls.

The ceiling seemed to be too high, and the walls looked endless. Light bounced around the room from the uneven windows scattered around. The floors were polished and sanded down. The only furniture in the room was a single wingback chair that sat in front of the upgraded fireplace. A disheveled bedroll was in the corner. It was clean and hollow.

The sparse kitchen and lack of personal touch left Cully speechless. There were a few habits that spoke of a man with military experience, but other than that, Cully wasn't able to profile the man at all. Usually he was good at reading people by a doing a quick catalogue of their possessions or their appearance. But Billy Voss didn't seem to have possessions.

He waited until a tall, well-dressed man entered the house from the back door. The man wiped his hands off onto a towel by the door and put on a smile so crooked it would have made a gambler proud.

Cully absorbed his surroundings. "Hello, neighbor. My name is Samuel McCullough. Just thought I'd drop by to see how the renovations were comin' along and to meet the newest addition to our fine community."

"Bill Voss," the man said as he extended his hand. Cully accepted it and maintained eye contact. "I haven't seen you around Durango, Mr. McCullough. Or else I would have introduced myself immediately. Pleasure to meet you, sir."

"I ain't anybody special, just tryin' to turn my farm into something worthwhile. I saw the potential of a thrivin' ranch when I purchased the land, but life out here is tough."

Cully noticed the spark of interest in Bill Voss's eyes when he mentioned his property. Yeah, Voss definitely made him think of leeches and shady deals made in dark alleyways.

Obviously, the hired guns weren't the only ones ignorant of his reputation and skills. No one else in the four corner states would mistake Cully as a local farmer.

"I'm always willing to help out a gentleman in need, Mr. McCullough. If you're willing to sell your land—"

"Absolutely not," Cully interrupted with a politeness he did not feel. "I'm just interested in learnin' what your intentions are in these parts. You ain't from Durango that's for sure. So what made you interested in takin' on the responsibilities of ownin' and operatin' a ranch?"

"Honestly?" Voss asked, genuine emotion on his face for the first time since Cully walked through the door. When no disagreement met his words, he continued. "My plans sound simple, but the overall goal is ambition. I plan to expand my ranch to be the largest in the state. Might even consider buying the entire town and some other territories over time." Voss took a seat in his wingback chair as one of his gunslingers poured him a glass of whiskey.

Cully scoffed amusingly. "You think the people of this town are just gonna let that happen? Let me give you some friendly advice. They ain't gonna just give up their homes."

"I expect there to be... resistance. But they won't have a choice. No one will stand in my way if they know what's best for them. I can be an easy man, but not when I'm denied."

Cully didn't like the way Billy Voss's mouth curled around the word *resistance*. One of the hired guns looked a little twitchy as he watched Cully with unblinking eyes. Cully tried his best to just grin and clench his teeth as he played the role of the friendly, neighborhood farmer. "The people of Durango won't just let somebody push them around and take their land. You won't just get resistance, Mr. Voss. They'll take a stand."

The hired gun that sized Cully up got braver as he reached for his pistol. He eased into a gunfighter stance and shouted,

"I don't take kindly to somebody threatenin' my boss. Quick draw. You and me. Right here. Winner gets yer land."

Cully faced the man with the thick Louisiana accent and pondered the circumstances. It seemed like too much to ask that somebody be willing to hold a decent conversation without threats of violence. He turned to Voss who tilted his head in a way that was similar to a hound dog listening for a rabbit.

Cully hadn't come here to fight someone desperate to make an impression. "Stand down, son. It ain't worth it unless you want to be pushin' up the daisies. We're just talkin' like old friends. Ain't nothin' to get worked up over."

The man refused to back down, his fingers twitching near his waist, as the other men in the room began to laugh. Even Voss looked amused. Well, it was time to show these scavengers that he was a man to take seriously.

"I'll tell you again, stand down. No one needs to get hurt today."

The others kept laughing, but the man who was ready to draw narrowed his eyes. Cully whipped his revolver out of the holster in the blink of an eye and fired a single shot into the man's leg before he got his own gun upholstered.

Cully bolted for the door. He used the momentum of his run to crash into the door, sending it toppling to the floor but keeping him upright. He tripped a bit but ran for Samson. A shout behind him caused the tiny hairs on the back of his neck to stand up. Shots were fired. He turned and returned fire as he ran.

"Go after him. I want to know who he is! Take him alive, or else I'll skin you myself!"

———————

Bullets pinged off the walls. Billy Voss stood up from his favorite chair and reached into the breast pocket of his suit. He used the white, silk swatch of cloth that had been neatly folded to wipe the sweat off his cheek. Another suit ruined by the idiocy of his men. As long as it was their bodies shielding him from the shooting, he couldn't care less.

But whoever Samuel McCullough really was, he was a dead man for sure. Billy Voss did not take rejection gracefully. Samuel McCullough had toyed with him, pretended to be someone he wasn't. Cunning games were what he loved best, but not when he was on the receiving end. He watched as the elusive man dashed across the yard toward his horse.

The useless, visionless mongrels Billy had hired kept firing well after Samuel McCullough was out of sight. Yes, he had expected resistance, but not an outright infiltration of his home. The man had slipped past his defenses with a harmless grin and a common story about being a struggling farmer with a dream of owning a ranch. Billy had been played for a fool.

When the banging, roaring mass of noise settled down to the clicking sounds of guns without ammunition, he took a deep breath to calm his anger. Samuel McCullough had somehow gotten away unscathed and without killing any of his men. On a better day, Billy would have been impressed.

Once the fury boiling in his veins subsided, he was able to address the worthless gunslingers circling his space. "Get yourselves cleaned up and looking presentable. I want three of you to go to town to find out who we're up against."

Billy's right-hand man, Ira Bennett, poured him another glass and said, "I'll go. We might need some more men to increase security. Whoever he is, he saw our faces, so we'll need to get people placed around town to keep an eye on things. Guys he won't suspect if he rides through."

Remy Logan, Billy's tracker, spoke up. "Do you think someone hired him to take a look at the place? Chances are he is not just some random citizen looking to do some good. The way he drew that revolver…"

The group went quiet.

Samuel McCullough was an unknown hindrance to Billy's plan. Even if he was as harmless as he had claimed to be, the man had made himself a threat to his plans just by showing up. "Remy, talk to Jerry at the store, see if anybody has been asking about us. Ira, you'll find me more men and drop by Denis Seeley's place."

"What do you want me to say when I get there?" Ira asked with his brow furrowed in apparent confusion. He was loyal, but not the smartest one of the bunch.

"I need you to issue some sort of threat—anything that will get him to rethink my proposal—but nothing violent. We don't need the sheriff banging on my—" Billy's words cut off when he looked at the shattered fragments of his front door. His entire body began to vibrate with pent up frustration. "Everybody, get out of my house. And send someone to fix my door, or else it's coming out of your pay."

The hired guns scampered like rats to obey his commands. Billy turned his head from side to side to relieve some tension in his neck. He pulled off his ruined suit to change into something just as ridiculously expensive. People wouldn't take him seriously if he didn't look the part.

Billy ambled out to the buckboard that waited on the other side of the property. He needed to pay a visit to a few of the ranches surrounding Durango. Although Samuel McCullough and Denis Seeley had turned down his offers, he was confident that other members of the community would be a little less bold and a little more desperate.

The world could think he was a wicked man who preyed on the helpless all they wanted—and they would be correct—but he was a man of many talents. Billy would make sure that they knew exactly what kind of man they were dealing with. Power and wealth were his endgame, and he intended to see his plan through to the end. No matter how many so-called innocent lives were caught in the crossfire. He would keep the peace for as long as it served his purpose, but eventually he wouldn't be able to stay his hand against insolence and insubordination.

Chapter 5

Four. Four times Billy Voss had been denied something in the last six hours. He had sent Remy into town after the incident with Samuel McCullough to dig up some information, but the entire community was a tight-lipped, united front dedicated to keeping him in the dark. Remy said the folk of Durango were surprised he had never heard of the man known as Cully, but they refused to give them any real information regarding the man's identity.

Billy felt like he had run into a brick wall as far as Cully was concerned, at least for now, so he focused the efforts of his men on getting his point across. Every time he offered one of the simpleminded landowners a fair price for their land, they all but laughed in his face. But Billy wasn't the sort of man to pull back when he got shoved. No, he was the sort that applied more force until the other side submitted to his will.

Ira tripped through the door just as Billy set down his glass of whiskey. The man sat on the floor with a long, drawn-out groan that caused Billy to frown. "What happened at the Seeley Ranch, Ira?" he asked.

"Well, there were a lot of townspeople out there helping him rebuild. They're making some decent progress, but I had to wait until nightfall so I wouldn't be seen."

"And?" Billy prodded.

"And Cully was there."

He squeezed the glass in his hand so hard it shattered in his fist. One of his men vying for his attention ran over and cleaned up the mess before offering him a towel. Billy didn't even acknowledge the gesture nor did he look up at any moment. His eyes practically burned into the side of Ira's face.

"I'm sorry, Billy. I wasn't able to send a threat, but I did find out some information about Cully. He didn't look like an ordinary farmer. Seemed like he was pretty close with Denis and his granddaughter. He did hourly walks around the place, but never the same path twice, so I couldn't really sneak past him."

"What else?"

"Searched his saddlebags when he finally settled in for the night." Ira reached into his pockets and pulled out a stack of letters tied together with twine. "Found these. Cully is some sort of big shot bounty hunter around here. There are letters from his sister Doris, a woman named Maria, and a few of his friends, along with several wanted posters."

Billy reached down and shuffled through the letters and contracts. "So Denis is an old friend of Cully's father?"

"That's what the most recent letter says. Denis blabbed about the fire. Cully must be looking into things and keeping an eye on the place."

"So the community protects him, his friends have risked their lives to keep him alive, he's a famous bounty hunter, and clearly he has never failed a contract. The man must be a saint. Samuel McCullough may become a problem which means we need to get our message across to these unsophisticated half-wits around here," Billy fumed. "Grab the boys and go round up some more men. I want four."

"You got it, boss. Four men with no ties, no ambitions, and empty pockets." Ira climbed to his feet and left quickly.

Billy stood up and crunched across the tiny shards of glass that still tinkled on the floor. He pressed his fingers to his temples and tried to relieve the growing headache behind his eyes. He didn't need another problem to deal with, especially one as experienced and determined as Cully. There were many things Billy Voss could look past, but he didn't like the thought of someone poking his nose in other people's business. Maybe he would leave town again soon, and Billy wouldn't have to deal with him interfering with his work.

But if some details in those letters were anything to go by, Cully wasn't an easy man to make disappear. Everything he did, he did it on his own time and he did it his way. Seemed like the bounty hunter had friends in very high places and some friends so low to the ground, they were practically beneath the surface.

Billy felt Remy grip his shoulder. "You okay, boss?"

"Why doesn't anyone want the money? It's more than what their land is worth, and yet they don't seem to care."

"Maybe they're more like you than you give them credit for. These don't seem like the type of people who really care about material things. They live off the land and work themselves down to the marrow. Perhaps if you offered them something that wasn't money..."

"And what do you suggest?" Billy asked as he quirked a skeptical brow and looked over his shoulder.

"Their families. We can use them as leverage. Either they give up their land or we make their lives miserable."

"I am not a man of violence. I'm a man of business."

"Well, sooner or later you'll have to make good on the threats you've been throwing around."

———————

Doris Hawes watched as her brother made his way down the long dirt road leading to her house. He rode on the back of Samson with the weight of the world on his shoulders. For the life of her, Doris could not understand why he insisted on living the life he had made for himself. She continued to watch his movements, noting the way he favored his left leg and how many times he stopped to take a long breath.

He may be one of the best bounty hunters in the entire west, but he wasn't immortal. Sooner or later, his actions were destined to catch up to him and Doris just wished that when that time came, he would have someone to go home to. Eventually he would have to retire at some point, right?

When he knocked on the door, Doris opened it without hesitation and stood to the side to let him in. He took a moment to just feel the warmth of the house before he turned to look at her. "Hey there, Doris Ann," Cully drawled.

"You mind telling me why you're limping, Sam?"

"Some of Billy Voss's men have been making threats to the ranchers in the area. Guess the gang didn't like me bein' there to defend the Harris family when they came knockin'. Got myself into a bit of a fistfight, but it ain't nothin' I can't handle." Cully waved off her worry with a slight wave of his hand.

Doris rolled her eyes but helped him remove his hat and boots. Once he was settled in one of the kitchen chairs, she began to prepare a pot of tea even though she knew Cully would have wanted something stronger to ease his pain. He was a good man who didn't imbibe all that often, but that didn't mean she would ever allow a drop of liquor in her home.

"Where's Ethan?" Cully asked while he peered around the modest little kitchen space.

"My husband went into town to speak with a man about a job. He should be back within the hour. Here, drink this." Doris bit the inside of her cheek to keep from laughing at his facial expression as he gulped down the aromatic tea. She couldn't hold it in much longer after his large body shuddered dramatically.

"You scrape this off the bottom of a boot? Here I thought you adored your big brother…"

"It was a gift I got from a woman who came here all the way from China. She told me it speeds up the healing process. I don't know if it's true, but a good cup of tea never hurt nobody."

"'Bout killed me just from the taste, so I don't know about the healin' part. Sure did wake me up though."

Doris sat down in the chair across from Cully with her own cup of tea. It smelled sort of sweet, but he was right: the taste was not something she would like to experience causally. She let out a little chuckle and met his gaze. Doris could see the spark of humor in his eyes. "Do you want to talk about it, Sam?"

"Talk about what?"

She rolled her eyes again. "The job you're working in town. You never did tell me what it was."

"I'm just doin' Denis Seeley a favor, that's all. It ain't really a job. He thinks Billy Voss had somethin' to do with the fire at his place. With all the threats and offers on property goin' around, he's worried people will get hurt."

"Do you believe him?"

Cully thought on that for a moment. He risked another sip of his tea before he answered. "After what I saw at Voss's spread, I'm more inclined than I was when I first agreed to look into things. He's got a bunch of single-minded plans."

"Like what?"

"Well, he's determined to buy up all the ranches around here, even mentioned buyin' the whole dang town. I'm not sure how much money he's got, but he said he was willin' to do whatever it takes to get what he wants. Sounded pretty ominous when he said it, but—"

"But you still don't have proof that he's the one who started the fire," Doris interjected. "He just came out of nowhere. I didn't know a single person in town who had heard of Billy Voss or his men until recently. Outsiders.... they tend to not be trusted as much by the people of Durango."

"No, you're right. Especially when they make an impression like Voss. Even Sheriff Lassiter said he didn't get a good feelin' about the man, and I trust his instincts."

The front door opened and Doris shouted, "We're in the kitchen!" followed by, "Don't forget to take off your boots!"

She looked over at Cully, who grinned from ear to ear at her delicately spoken commands. When Ethan finally joined them in the kitchen, Doris felt the love of her family surrounding her. Her husband leaned down and gave her a swift peck on the lips before she could protest. Doris fanned her flaming cheeks and swatted Ethan playfully on the arm. "You're in a good mood."

"I come home every day to a lovely wife, a nice home, and a bright future ahead of me. I'm a simple man, darlin'. Don't take much to keep me happy, you do just fine."

"Why don't you sit down with Sam and talk about your meeting while I start fixing supper?" Doris returned her husband's affection and rounded the table to begin cooking. Her skirts brushed just above the floor as she hummed happily, moving around the small kitchen.

"So how'd your meetin' go?"

"Well, after Doris made me promise to quit the mines, I knew I had to start looking for work. If we're going to start a family soon, we'll need all the money we can get. There were a few offers today," Ethan answered.

"What were they?"

"Sheriff Lassiter offered me a position as a deputy. But I know how Doris feels about firearms and that sort of thing. Then Archie down at the saloon offered me some work behind the bar, but that's just not my atmosphere. Decided to take the job working the forge down at the blacksmith shop."

Doris was happy with her husband's choice. It wasn't an easy job, but it would allow Ethan more time around the farm while working some much-needed hours. "I was thinking of getting a job too," she admitted.

Her brother and her husband both looked at her from over the countertop. She could see it in their eyes that they wanted to object, but she turned her back to them before they could say anything. "Just a simple job down at the schoolhouse. It'll give me something to do while we work toward getting the farm in shape before the warmer weather comes."

"I think you'd make a fine teacher, Doris Ann."

"Thank you, Sam."

Chapter 6

Billy Voss gently knocked on the front door of the large house that sat upon the landscape of the Montoya Ranch. It was one of the largest spreads he had seen in the Durango region, which meant he was eager to get his hands on the deed. His men stood a few feet behind him, their revolvers on display as the door finally cracked open.

It was early in the morning, not long after dawn, when Felix Lowery peeked his head through the opening. Billy wasn't a fool; he knew there was a shotgun just beyond the door that still separated their bodies. Word in town was that Felix married up with Ruby Montoya and inherited the land after his wife's father passed away. The ranch had seen better days since falling under new ownership, so Billy wanted to make an offer that would ease their burdens—kind man that he was.

"Morning, neighbor." Billy's voice took on a note that was as sweet as honey. "Sorry to wake you, but I was wondering if you had a moment to chat."

"Come back when we..." Felix Lowery's words died on his tongue swiftly as Billy's men stepped forward in a blatant display of dominance. His face turned pale as he stepped aside to invite them in. "Mind if I ask what this is about?" Felix asked as he set the shotgun aside. He was outnumbered, so it wouldn't do him any good to use it. Subconsciously he glanced to the ceiling.

Billy Voss shook with mocking laughter. "Don't worry about your wife, Mr. Lowery. We aren't here to hurt anybody. My name is Billy Voss, and I'm looking to acquire some land here in the Durango area." He impatiently snapped his fingers until one of his men handed him the documented proposal. The number was more than reasonable. "Take a look at what I have to offer and talk it over with that pretty wife of yours. If I don't hear back from you within three days..."

The clicking sound of the hammer being pulled back on a pistol was loud like thunder in the quiet morning. Felix lifted his hands in surrender and stepped back until he was pressed against the wall. "Please—"

"Three days," Billy interrupted. "After that, I'll come back, and I'll take everything that you have by force, and you won't be able to stop it. I don't make an offer twice."

He waited, watching as the man before him cowered at the sight of him.

Billy inhaled deeply and breathed in the smell of fear as the intoxicating high of power rushed through his body. "You have a nice day, Mr. Lowery."

The next six visits went in a similar fashion. Some slight resistance that was met by the cold promise of violence that dripped from Billy Voss's lips. Although some of his men doubted that he would follow through with the threats, Billy meant every word. They threatened every farm and ranch within a twenty-mile radius from Durango.

He walked over to his horse and leaned up against his side as he checked off another name on his list. The plans he had in mind for Colorado required intricate details that needed to be managed regularly. Billy didn't trust anyone else to keep track of the accounts, purchases, rations, payroll, or even the offers floating around. He kept dates and records of every interaction he made with others, no matter how insignificant they seemed at the time.

It was his way of keeping people unsure of exactly how much wealth he had amassed over the years. The Pinkertons could investigate all they wanted, but they would never find anything. Their efforts were wasted. The Voss family, especially Billy's father, had mastered the art of embezzlement, extortion, and secrecy long ago. The knowledge was passed down from generation to generation, leaving no trail behind. It was the very lifeblood of his lineage.

To his surprise as he checked off important markers on his map, Samuel "Cully" McCullough approached them just outside of the Montoya property. The arrogant smirk on the bounty hunter's face irked Billy. "To what do I owe the pleasure, Mr. McCullough?" he prompted.

"You wouldn't happen to be payin' Felix and Ruby a visit, now would y'all? Heard you've been makin' some pretty big claims round here, Voss."

The muscle in Billy's jaw twitched as he struggled to maintain his composure. The tone of Cully's voice sounded like a father speaking to a petulant son. It was belittling, and Billy wanted to remove that look of amusement off the man's face. "How's the family, Mr. McCullough?"

There. The uncertainty and suspicion returned to Cully's eyes as that crooked grin disappeared behind a blank expression. Billy reveled in the fact that he had succeeded in poking at one of Cully's weak spots. "Never you mind about my family, Voss. Just came to warn you that folks are gettin' tired of your high-handed threats on their lives. Keep your men in check and keep your business clean, or else you'll have me to deal with. We clear?"

"Not quite. I've got another name on my list to visit by the end of the week. Then I'll be heading out of town for a while."

———————

Cully looked down at the man who wore a suit in the middle of a Colorado winter and shook his head. He hated to admit it, but Voss had zeroed in on his only weakness. Not many people knew his and Doris's history, especially outsiders. So when Voss had mentioned his family, Cully had seen the red fires of damnation flickering in his vision. He would not hesitate to kill for his family.

However, Voss had unintentionally walked right into Cully's plan. The man was too smart to leave enough evidence to warrant an arrest, so Cully would have to use other methods to draw out a confession or even catch Voss in the act. He just had to make sure that the businessman took the bait.

"I reckon you've got your eye on my family's land. But mark my words... My sister ain't to be trifled with, Voss."

Billy Voss's expression was just as predictable as the laugh that followed Cully's words. "I'll consider them marked."

Good, no doubt Voss had seen his threat as a challenge. That was exactly what he had hoped for. If Voss and his men attacked Doris's place openly in retaliation, it would be enough to buy the Pinkertons enough time to gather more evidence in their investigation or give Cully enough time to prove he had started the fire. Either way, Voss was a bad seed, and he needed to rid Durango of any threats he could.

"Just take my advice. You ain't gonna get the people of Durango to submit their land to you willingly under a bunch of threats. Try talkin' to people like they ain't beneath you."

"I've offered them all a fair price. I haven't done anything that would warrant such bitter resentment from the community. They may have their assumptions on who I am and what I plan to do with their land, but they have no idea who I am." Voss cocked his head to the side and said, "And neither do you. That scares you, doesn't it, Mr. McCullough? You finally found the one man you can't figure out."

When Cully didn't answer, Voss continued to taunt him.

"That's it, isn't it? You're stumped. You like puzzles, Mr. McCullough, but you don't like mysteries. You investigate, track down the bad guy, and then you get justice—but this time… it's different."

"You're all the same," Cully muttered. "All talk."

"No, I don't think so. This time you can't investigate because there's no crime. You can't track down a bad guy that doesn't exist. And you can't get justice, because there's no evidence. All you have is a vendetta against my business and me. I'm standing in front of you, holding all the cards."

"Threatenin' people—"

Voss shouted, thoroughly cutting off Cully's words. "Last I checked, talking to people wasn't a crime! I show up, I chat, I make an offer, and I leave. They interpret my words however they like. I'm just here to build an empire."

"*No one will stand in my way if they know what's best for them*," Cully quoted. "That's what you said to me the day we met, ain't it? Sounded like a threat to me."

"It was a provocation, Mr. McCullough."

"You ain't nothin' but an oppressor tryin' to bully his way across the west. But we've dealt with men like you more often than you're aware, Voss. And we won't tolerate your *provocations* much longer. If you find yourself tempted to even come near my sister's property, you won't like the results." Cully clucked his tongue and pushed Samson on toward the ranch.

He ignored Voss's shouts of profanity.

The visit with Felix and Ruby went as well as could be expected. Felix was scared silent, refusing to tell Cully what he and Voss discussed. If the community didn't band together and drive Voss out of town, there might not be anything left for him to do besides wait. But the newcomers and their threats looming above people's heads had everybody too scared to leave their land unattended. Denis Seeley feared his fire had been a warning to everybody who would deny Voss.

And while some folks held their ground, Cully had heard the many names that had bent to the will of Voss and his men. Not that he blamed them for keeping their families safe, but Cully wished there was more he could do for them.

As much as people would like to think that Voss was all talk and no walk, he wasn't so easily convinced. The businessman had a calm about him that made Cully nervous. No one knew who the man really was, so there was no way to predict any of his moves. There may be some subtle similarities between Voss and a few of the men he had hunted down over the years, but there was an unknown element about him that caused Cully some concern.

There was no such thing as a man without a past. It may take a while, but Cully was determined to uncover the truth about Billy Voss. He rode on the back of Samson until he reached Durango. There was a potent atmosphere of exuberance as well as apprehension that settled over everyone. Many people looked up and smiled or waved in his direction as he passed.

He would try his best to keep the community safe and help in any way he could to make sure that Billy Voss did not make good on the threats he threw about recklessly.

Sheriff Lassiter waved Cully down and offered to buy him a drink at the saloon which he agreed to. They needed to talk anyway. Some discussion should be had about increasing the security at some outlying homesteads so that no one was caught unaware. They didn't need another mysterious fire to happen, someone else losing their livelihoods.

"I wish we could bring him in on charges for the threats, but no one is willin' to file a report. Even if they did, it wouldn't do much to hold him. We ain't got nothin' for certain to bring Voss down. Intimidation ain't no crime," Sheriff Lassiter grumbled.

"I've run into the same issue, myself. He's careful. And if this is how he operated before comin' here, who's to say he didn't do it somewhere else, too. The difference is this is our town, and we're aware of it. He could have been doin' this for years for all we know. Too slick to get caught..."

"Uh oh."

"What?" Cully asked with a frown.

"I know what that look in your eyes means, Cully. He's gotten to you a bit, hasn't he? You're about to do somethin' reckless. But before you do, think about Doris..."

Chapter 7

Cully sat at the not-so-fancy restaurant attached to one of the local hotels and ordered a serving of steak and potatoes. Doris and Ethan came in, and he smiled fondly as Ethan brushed the snow from Doris's coat. She gave her husband an adoring, dimpled smile and sat across from Cully. Once they were settled in, he waited for them to get warm before he spoke.

"Now, you know I've been investigatin' the fire at Denis Seeley's and the threats from Voss. But there ain't no way we can put an end to all of this without catchin' him in the act. Sheriff Lassiter agrees," he explained. "I set a trap that I think will work, but I know you ain't gonna like it, Doris."

"Will it keep the town safe?"

"You haven't even heard what the plan is..."

"And I don't need to," Doris said. "I trust you, Sam. No one has kept Durango as safe as you have. And as much as I hate the thought of you putting yourself in danger, I can't let anyone else lose their homes to this anymore. It isn't right."

Cully reached over and held his sister's hand. "And you always do the right thing."

"At least I try to. So now that I've agreed. Let's talk about this while you finish your dinner."

When his plate was set down in front of him, Cully kicked himself for not ordering a beer with his meal. But then he looked at Doris and knew she would not approve, so he settled for a cup of coffee. "So I spoke with Voss and let him know that you weren't to be trifled with. He took it as a challenge, just as I knew he would. Now, there's a chance he and his boys are gonna try to retaliate."

"And you think they'll try to attack the house?" Ethan asked. "Is there a way to defend ourselves?"

"I'll be stayin' in the barn until this all falls into place. Checkin' the fence line and keepin' an eye on everything. I won't leave y'all unprotected, and I'll keep my rifles in the barn with me. But I want to at least know that you'll be willin' to defend yourselves if this goes wrong..." Cully cast a pointed look at Doris. He knew exactly how she felt about violence of any sort, but there may come a time when she would have to set aside her beliefs. She could pray for forgiveness later as long as she was safe. "Doris Ann."

"I know what you're asking, Sam."

"But I need an answer. Are you willin' to protect yourself and your home, if need be?" He watched how she avoided his piercing gaze and fidgeted with the sleeve of her dress. Cully knew he was asking much of his sister, but he couldn't stand the thought of what might happen to her if Voss and his men slipped through his defenses.

"All right, Sam. If and *only if* they are a threat to my life or Ethan's life or your life. Only then will I resort to... to violence. You're the only family I have at the moment, and I don't want to lose either of you to something so foolish as greed."

Cully released Doris's hand and set about clearing his plate. The newly married couple changed the subject to what they envisioned for their future. He was content with just listening as he ate, eager to feel some sort of normalcy. The domesticity of their conversation did not fall on deaf ears.

He wanted nothing but to give Doris the life she deserved. There was something about the wistful look in her eyes that said that some part of her believed the things they talked about would only remain a dream. Cully wished he had the sweet words of his mother or the years of wisdom of his father. Something to offer his sister to ease her worries.

Sensing the shift in conversation once again, he thought about any good news he had to share. There wasn't much involving him in particular, but he had a few friends who had been blessed recently. "Charlotte and Wolf are thinkin' on headin' up north to get married. They say the people up there are more tolerant of nontraditional families."

"That's wonderful news!" Doris said passionately.

"It is. Also got word from Mateo Rodriguez finally. Says he found Maria all the way down near the border of Mexico and California. A gang leader named Raúl Bernal that Mateo owed a debt to had taken her for ransom. Apparently, Maria put up a fight they hadn't expected. She nearly took out the entire gang in secret before Mateo even showed up to take care of the leader."

"Are they on their way back to Cheyenne? Perhaps we could pay them a short visit when they return. At least so I can thank her for saving your life so many times."

Cully could have hugged Doris. Only his sister would look past the worst parts of his story and see an opportunity to thank someone. "I'm not sure Maria will want to go back right away. Eventually she'll want to get La Rosa up and runnin' again, but Mateo said they most likely would stay with Grace and Wesley until they get settled down a bit. But Maria is strong. She'll make it."

"You admire her?" Ethan urged with a smile. "You never speak so comfortably of a woman, Cully. It's hard to imagine."

"Ain't too many women out there that would sew a dyin' man back together on her kitchen table while scoldin' him for gettin' injured in the first place. She threatened to kill me about as many times as she saved my life."

Doris laughed softly. "Now I must meet her."

"Yeah, you would like her. Charlotte and Grace as well. They're some extraordinary women I've had the privilege of knowin'. They've become family rather quickly." The smile on Cully's face was genuine. He couldn't help but think fondly of the strong, resourceful women he had met in the past few months. They were like sisters to him. And Caden, Wesley, Wolf, and the others were as close to being brothers as Ethan.

"Well, any of your family are welcome in our home for the Christmas season. It would be nice to have a big shindig like the ones Mama and Daddy used to have at the church."

He never really considered there would be a day when his family on the road would meet his blood family. But he didn't see anything wrong with it. He just hoped the spitfire women he associated with didn't influence Doris too much. He much preferred her passive ways. "That sounds nice, Doris Ann."

"Maybe Alice can come along as well..."

"Alice Seeley?" Cully asked with a frown.

"She speaks very highly of you, Sam." By the shy flush on Doris's face and Ethan's knowing smirk, Cully knew he wasn't the only McCullough laying traps around Durango. Doris clearly had her mind set on matchmaking.

"Look here, young lady—"

"I'm not telling you to go off and just get married. I just want you to consider your options. We've known the Seeleys for many years, and it would not be bad for you to ponder courting someone. From what I hear, there isn't a woman from Colorado to Alabama that would turn down the opportunity."

Cully's own blush rivaled Doris's, as well as anybody else within a twenty-mile spread. He looked down at the last few bites of potatoes on his plate and cleared his throat. He wanted to protest. He wanted to tell Doris to focus on her own life and let him worry about his, but he couldn't bring himself to dash her hopes. Doris would forever believe he was worthy of a better life even if he knew otherwise.

"I ain't makin' no promises, Doris. But I'll keep my mind open to the possibility of a courtship. Might not be anyone special and it might not work out, but I'll try."

"Thank you, Sam. I just want you to be as happy as Ethan and I. There are a lot of blessings that come with marriage."

Doris was as stubborn as he was, but Cully had never mastered the big doe eyes she had at her disposal to get whatever she wanted out of her big brother. He laughed through his nose and paid for his meal before they left the restaurant together. He walked over to Samson and patted his side as he looked past Ethan and met his sister's stare.

"Get home safe. I'll be there in about an hour or so to get everythin' set up."

"I'll fix up the loft in the barn for you, Sam. Be safe."

———————

Billy Voss tossed and turned on his bedroll on the floor of his ranch house. Memories of the war played havoc on his mind as he struggled to get through even an hour's worth of sleep. The fatigue of running an operation almost entirely on his own started to wear on his body. He began making progress a few days back. Billy secured several properties neighboring his own land, which he already had men guarding in case the former owners decided they wanted out of the agreement.

Not that there was a surefire way out of a deal with Billy Voss, but he was often surprised when people thought to double-cross him. No one could swindle a crook like him. Not even Cully although the man had tried his best to intimidate Billy the day before. There was a fight in the bounty hunter that he truly admired, but at the same time, this wasn't the sort of fight Cully was used to. Billy was sure about that.

Everything seemed to come so easily for the illustrious only son of the beloved Reverend Benjamin McCullough of Durango, Colorado. It took a while, but they had figured out the only way to learn anything of value about Cully was to ask at the church in town. The sister, Doris, was even harder to investigate than the man himself. Most likely it was due to Cully's insistence that the entire town protect her.

Sibling love and respect wasn't something practiced by the Voss family. At a young age, Billy had traveled around the country with his father and grandfather, pulling off deals and filling up a book of favors. He loved the feeling that came with knowing that others were in debt to him, even back then. He could reach out to any name in his book of favors, and they would have no choice but to carry out his bidding in the fear of retaliation. That was power.

He stared up at the endlessness above him and watched the moonlight filter in through the windows. Billy felt the cold of winter reaching toward his back through the floor. He didn't sleep with a fire going, uncomfortable with the warmth that heated his skin. No, the cold was the only thing welcome during his time of rest. His men knew better than to disturb him after sunset.

Or so he had hoped. The quiet knock on his door had Billy clenching his jaw.

"Hey, Boss!" Ira yelled as Billy silently vowed to shoot the man sometime in the near future.

He jumped to his feet from the cold floor and took a moment to watch the breath leave his mouth in a stream of silken smoke as he calmed himself down. Billy walked over to the newly repaired door and opened it. "You know I hate to be bothered, Ira. What is it?"

"We found the farm where Cully's sister and her husband live. It's a nice little plot with land for crops or even an orchard of some kind. There were a lot of trees. Even a freshwater well on the property."

"Tell the boys to round up and be ready; we'll pay the lovely Mrs. Doris Hawes a little visit in a few days."

Chapter 8

For three days, Cully slept in the barn's loft, lying in wait for Voss to show up with his men. He cleaned and prepared his guns regularly as he watched through the opened window. Cully polished his Sharps and propped his Winchester '76 up against the wall beneath the window.

In addition to his Colt .44 Peacemaker, he had another smaller handgun, two throwing knives, and his usual hunting blade. There were several cases of shells neatly stacked within reach. From the vantage point, he could see out over the land surrounding the house, in case they didn't make a direct approach for the attack.

Cully expected Voss to be direct, but so far, the man had demolished his expectations. He was not used to going up against a real businessman with achievable goals, only outlaws with farfetched aspirations. If Cully's strategy to draw him into a trap failed, Voss would succeed in claiming much of the land in the area. Which would mean that his and Doris's hometown would change forever.

So many people were already forced to leave their homes after the hopelessness of their financial troubles was too much for them to withstand. Billy Voss appeared out of nowhere like a man with all the answers to their problems. But there were a few families and homesteads in the area that would not bend so easily. He was proud to call Durango his hometown.

Many of the people of Durango had been there long before it blossomed into the town it was known to be. The history of the land and its people were soaked into the earth beneath the settlement, bringing strength to both.

"Everything all right, Sam?" Doris asked. He looked up and gave her a gentle smile and motioned for her to get comfortable. She often came to chat before going to bed, often just to make sure that he promised to eat his supper before it got too cold. Doris had the heart of an angel.

"Just about. I'll finish up here and be in the house for supper shortly. Y'all head on to bed when you want to. Thanks for gettin' this place lookin' nice for me."

"You're my brother. Couldn't stand the thought of you sleeping on a cold floor when I could do something about it. Life does not always have to be as difficult as you make it, Sam." Doris knelt down beside Cully and looked out the window. Her homemade clothing was immaculate and perfectly tailored. She had wanted to make a good impression earlier in the day when she went down to the schoolhouse.

Cully knew she nearly ran herself into the ground trying to keep up a household as well as handle all the activities down at the church. Doris wouldn't take no for an answer after setting her mind on being a schoolmarm. But she couldn't hide the small, puffy bags beneath her eyes or the many headaches she tried to nurse in private—at least not from him. Cully understood that drive to mean something.

He knew the signs of restless nights and long days. It had been his reality since the day he left home. He never wanted Doris to miss a night's rest or a hot meal, but he also knew he could not control her life. Even though she had married Ethan and became Doris Ann Hawes, to Cully she would always be a McCullough.

And McCulloughs were headstrong and capable.

"I appreciate you tryin' to take care of me, Doris Ann. But I want you to take care of yourself first. Ain't no need for the both of us to lose sleep," Cully said as he removed one of his jackets and placed it over her shoulders. At least the walls of the barn loft kept the wind from getting to them. "Only take on what you're able to handle. I know you want to help people, especially with all of this Billy Voss nonsense happenin', but you don't need any complications if you're lookin' into startin' a family soon. No need to stress."

"You're right. Maybe after things are back to normal, I'll be able to sleep better. I don't know how you do it, Sam," Doris sighed as she worried her hands in her lap. "It feels like every day I get more fragile, but you seem to only be getting stronger, even though you hardly sleep through the night.

"After a while it all becomes second nature. I barely think about it most of the time. Thinkin' bout the wrong things can be dangerous for a bounty hunter. There are times when I don't eat or sleep for days, but I can't let it distract me from what's important. On the road, there ain't as many amenities to be had. I have to keep my mind sharp and my instincts—"

Cully heard a horse whine. From the distance it echoed from and the direction, he knew it wasn't Samson or one of

Ethan's horses. No, that was from down the dirt road. He quickly loaded the spare Peacemaker and pressed it into the palm of Doris's hand. Her eyes widened with unspoken fear as her jaw dropped low. He shook his head and wrapped her fingers around the grip. "Run out back, get into the house, and hide in the cellar. Don't make any noise, and if you see or hear anythin', do not come out."

Doris trembled. "What is it? Are they here?"

"I need you to concentrate! Do as I say, please. Take Ethan with you and tell him to grab that shotgun I strapped to the underside of the kitchen table. No! No arguing! I know you don't like guns, but you promised. Remember?"

When Doris finally nodded her head and rushed to carry out his request, Cully watched until she ran into the house from the back door. He thought they would have had more time before the attack, but he had been wrong. A line of men on horseback rode in perfect formation as they approached the farm. Cully reached for his Sharps, doused the oil lamp, and blended into the shadows of the barn.

The moon provided the only light, and even that couldn't penetrate the darkness he had shrouded himself with. He counted one, two, three, four… dang, there were seven men, including Billy Voss himself. Cully thought it was a bit much for a simple visit, but he suspected the businessman didn't go anywhere without at least two men for his own protection.

Cully was actually surprised that he showed up to the fight. He half expected the man to remain anonymous in all the chaos, but his ego must have demanded his presence. Voss didn't lead the mob. He rode near the back. No doubt, wanting to witness the destruction they intended for himself, not knowing he walked right into Cully's trap. He sent a silent prayer for Doris's safety.

———————

Billy Voss sat astride his horse. The men he had hired to burn down the Hawes Farm carried torches. Ira took a swig of whiskey from his almost empty bottle before tucking a handkerchief down its neck and lighting it on fire. He howled loudly into the night. Before Ira could toss the flaming bottle at the farmhouse, a bullet whistled through the air and struck him in the chest.

The horses panicked and bucked a few of the riders. From somewhere on the property, more shots rang through the air as Billy watched another one of his men go down. He didn't know where the shots had come from, but he didn't care. "Open fire!" he shouted.

A spray of gunfire vaulted toward the farmhouse and the barn. Glass from the windows shattered and flew across the porch as bullets ripped through the walls. Voss finally lifted his hand to halt the attack. When the merciless onslaught came to a silence, he called out to Cully. "I know that's you, McCullough."

"Surrender, Voss. Or this ain't gonna end well for you."

Billy chortled in pretend laughter.

"Last chance. Drop your guns and face me like a man, or we settle this my way. What kind of coward brings a mob to burn down the home of unsuspectin' civilians?"

Billy didn't respond to the jab with his words. He lit another torch and threw it into the barn. Fire exploded as the flames licked at every dry surface before it came to a full blaze. This time his laughter was genuine as he watched the scene with profound amusement. Sooner or later, the people of Durango would realize that he made good on his threats. What better way to prove that than by using Cully McCullough as an example?

They knew who he was now. He had been seen starting the fire, so there was no use in backing down. The odds were still in his favor as he and his men outnumbered Cully five to one. Suddenly, gunfire was returned from the inside of the house. Cold fury clenched in his chest as the sound of a shotgun joined the volley. He hadn't expected to kill anyone on this raid, but if it came down to him or somebody else... Billy had no problem crossing that line.

But whoever had been shooting from the farmhouse had no ill intentions. Their shots were aimed at the legs, meant to disarm more than kill. While his men were more than willing to die in order to fulfill their debts to him, Billy wouldn't sit around and wait for all of them to get picked off.

———————

Cully's heart sank the first time he heard the shotgun go off. He fastened himself with ammunition bags and slung his Winchester over his shoulder by the strap. He jumped down to the first level of the barn and opened the back door to release the animals. He ignored the twinge in his right leg as the animals ran.

A fierce wind blew through the barn and fed the flames.

The bite of the winter air felt thin and heavy in his lungs at the same time as he dashed for cover. A barrage of gunfire followed his every move, as he hoped and wished that Doris had made it to the cellar, grateful that Ethan wanted to buy him enough time to escape the barn. A quick look over his shoulder and Cully was able to see where Voss had been sitting idle while the others defended him. Coward. Either that or the man's arrogance just surpassed all logical thinking. Cully propped the barrel of his Winchester against a pile of firewood and took aim. He pulled the trigger. *Bang!*

One of the hired guns went down. By the frightened look on Voss's face, Cully assumed it had been one of his top guys. Probably someone he had traveled to Colorado with. Even so, Cully watched as Voss's cowardice had him tucking tail and heading for safety. The gunfire must have alerted the neighbors because Sheriff Lassiter and two of the town's deputies rode into the fight to take care of the stragglers.

Cully whistled through his fingers, and Samson ran up beside him. With one quick, fluid action while the horse was still in motion, he shoved his foot into the stirrup and hoisted himself into the saddle. He took off in pursuit of Voss with a curse on his lips and anger in his heart.

No one attacked his family and got away with it.

Voss's eastern roots began to show as Cully realized how easy the tracks were to follow. He must not have spent much time outside of cities or settlements to know anything about hiding from someone on his trail. Well, Cully was more than willing to teach him that valuable lesson tonight.

Chapter 9

Doris heard the sound of her husband's voice beckoning her out of the cellar where she hid near the back of the room. The damp, musty walls soaked into her dress as she tried to press herself against the wall, as though she hoped to disappear into the stone. The cellar door opened, and light streamed down as Ethan's face came into view.

She was relieved to see his shining blue eyes against suntanned skin and dark hair. Even after almost a year of marriage, he still caused her heartbeat to quicken, as butterflies danced across her nerves. And when he gave her that beautiful, reassuring smile, Doris couldn't help but to walk into his arms.

He rubbed soothing circles over her back and ushered her to the main floor of the house. She never felt safer than she did in that moment with his arms wrapped around her shoulders.

Sheriff Jake Lassiter gave her a tightlipped grin and motioned for her to take a seat.

Ethan readied a pot of hot water to prepare her a cup of tea. Doris loved her husband. The days had been tough on both of them. She could see the strain in his muscles and the worry behind his brilliant stare. More than a day's worth of stubble dusted his cheeks and jaw, making his youthful appearance more mature than it really was. His hand brushed against her fingers as he handed her a cup of steaming tea, causing Doris to blush profusely and avert her gaze.

"Thank you," she whispered for his ears only.

Ethan pressed a kiss to Doris's temple and took a seat beside her. Doris instantly reached over and grasped his hand with her fragile, graceful fingers.

Sheriff Lassiter cleared his throat and spoke calmly. "Sorry to bother you with this, Doris."

"It's all right, Sheriff," she responded quietly.

"Most of the men left behind were arrested just now and taken into town under arson and extortion charges. Billy Voss got away, but your brother is trackin' him down as we speak. I hope Cully brings him in alive, but we don't know what sort of tricks Voss might have up his sleeves."

"Sam will bring him in alive. Voss didn't kill anyone or do anything particularly violent. My brother isn't a cruel man. I have faith that he'll bring him in kicking and screaming." Doris was certain. She could see the hesitance in the sheriff's eyes, but she knew Cully.

Yes, Voss had threatened her life and her future by attempting to set their home on fire, but there wasn't an unreasonable bone in her brother's body. Logically, he knew Billy Voss didn't deserve to die for his crimes.

Cully would see that the man was sent to a proper trial, and a full investigation into his activities would be launched, but he wouldn't risk further damnation on his soul for pettiness. And that was exactly what Billy Voss's actions were: petty.

The tips of Doris's fingers casually touched the wedding ring on her husband's hand. She knew the guilt of shooting a gun in their home would come crashing down on him once the adrenaline settled. She had her beliefs after all. But she hoped he understood that she could never fault him for trying to save the life of her only living blood relative.

There were few things in her life that meant as much to her as Cully did, so she prayed that he could see the appreciation and forgiveness she desperately wanted him to notice. Ethan pressed a kiss to her knuckles and nodded.

"I hope you're right, Doris," Sheriff Lassiter huffed. "Everybody in Durango knows how protective Cully is of you. It's a shame Voss and his boys didn't listen when they had the chance. We could have spared those three lives lost today."

"But they would have gotten away with their crimes. Sam explained how important it was to put Voss behind bars. Many men have been led astray by the temptation of greed. I will keep them in my prayers when I go to church this Sunday. We hope to see you there."

The sheriff smiled. "Wouldn't miss it for the world. Lookin' forward to those cookies you always bring."

Doris's laughter bubbled up as the respected lawman patted his belly and gave her a playful wink. She was happy to be surrounded by the genuine people of their community, and she hoped to see even brighter days ahead for them all.

Sheriff Lassiter left not too long after their discussion. Doris and Ethan walked him to the front door and decided it would be best if they stayed in town. Apart from some broken windows and bullet holes in the walls, not much damage had been done to the main house. But the barn was burned to the ground, and the livestock was scattered across the land.

Doris tried to set her mind at ease knowing that the people of Durango would assist them if they asked for help, but her heart ached with uncertainty. She knew Cully would try his best to return with Billy Voss in custody, but she didn't trust that he would do so and keep himself safe in the process. Samuel McCullough was a very complex man, and he often placed the well-being of others above his own.

Ethan helped Doris onto the buckboard and guided them to town in the early hours of the morning. The cold settled into her bones and caused her teeth to chatter, but Ethan's tight grasp on her hand kept her grounded. It took less than half an hour to reach Durango and another twenty minutes to get settled into a room comfortably. Bless his heart, Ethan knew Doris would not sleep knowing Cully was out in the cold hunting down Voss. He didn't pressure her; he silently cared for his wife while she worried over her brother.

"He knows how important he is to us, right? Sam wouldn't do anything foolish, would he?" she asked with a slight tremor in her lovely voice.

"Cully knows, Doris. If he feels like he needs to find redemption, we can't stand in his way. Only a sign from God will change his course of action. It's not our place."

"He just…" Doris closed her eyes against the tears that wet her flaming cheeks. "He takes on everyone else's problems and carries the burden for himself. But who does the same for him? Who will be there for Sam when he needs it?"

"You heard him the other night. There are people he has met on the road that risked their lives for him. He is surrounded by love and support. It may take time for Cully to see it, but when he does, he will know just how blessed he is."

Doris's wavering smile curved tenderly. "When did you get so wise? I remember the shy young man who used to chase after me with hearts in his eyes and flowers clutched in his hands like it was yesterday."

"I became wise somewhere around the time you finally told me that you loved me. A good woman is what turns a boy into a man, not the struggle of the life he lived. But the grace and beauty bestowed upon his life by God's greatest creation." Ethan wrapped his arms around Doris and held her tight. She listened to the steady beat of his heart and let the contentment and protection wash over her. "Cully will be fine, Doris."

Cully lowered himself from the saddle slowly, mindful of his leg that still felt irritated after the jump from the barn loft. He knelt down carefully and brushed his fingers against the dark, snow-dusted tracks from a horse going off in an odd direction. There were no settlements or lodgings anywhere in the area, which meant Voss had tried to set up camp without the proper supplies.

The only thing the pampered businessman would find out in the wild would be some coyote, bobcats, mountain lions, or the occasional black bear. Voss had only carried a revolver during the attack from what Cully could tell—obviously he never intended to need a firearm. But a small handgun would barely be effective against some dangerous carnivores native to these unclaimed parts of Colorado.

If the cause weren't so important, Cully would think this hunt was a waste of his time and skill. It was almost too easy to follow the broken twigs, disturbed foliage, and obvious trail that led to wherever Voss was holed up at. Cully knew the area, and he knew that just east of where he stood, there was an old mining cave that had collapsed several years back. It wouldn't be cavernous enough to be in danger of another rockslide, but it would be plenty deep to allow a bit of coverage from the wind for a few hours.

The smell of smoke still burned Cully's nose as disappointment sank in his gut like a stone tossed into a river. Shimmering rays of sunlight peeked through the bare trees of the surrounding forest, staining the sky with yellow and gray strokes of color. A chilling breeze blew across the back of his neck before Cully lifted the collar of his jacket against the wind. His fingers were stiff as they gripped the horn and used it to pull his large body back into the saddle. Samson sidestepped a bit.

Once he righted his posture, Cully continued through the woods, following the confused trail of a man who didn't have even the slightest idea of where he was headed. It would have been humorous on any other occasion, but Cully couldn't see past the anger that threatened to consume him when he thought about how close Doris came to getting injured.

He wanted to blame himself. If Cully hadn't lured Voss into the trap, he would never have known that Doris was his

Achilles heel. He had left his one weakness out in the open. For once he hadn't just put himself in the line of fire, he put the thing he loved most in this world directly in front of his enemy and practically dared the man to react.

Doris would never accuse him of such thoughtlessness, but that didn't mean Cully didn't feel guilty for the barn burning down or the house getting peppered with gunfire. He had enough things he blamed himself for, so he didn't have a problem adding to the list. No matter how pointless it was to dwell on the past, Cully wanted to remember his mistakes so he didn't repeat them.

His sister constantly told him to let things go and move on from the past, but how could he? Cully's entire life had been built upon the foundation of retribution for something that happened nearly a decade ago. If he hadn't let it go by now, he didn't think he ever would. But he was fine with that. Remembering kept him focused on what was important. It gave him a reason to stay true to his vow.

There was no doubt that while he made progress toward his goals, his faith had suffered the backlash. But he didn't give up hope, for he still believed in salvation. If he didn't, that meant that his vow meant nothing. And that scared Cully more than almost anything else in life. He needed to believe. He needed hope that salvation was within his reach.

Chapter 10

Billy Voss huddled as close to the back of the small cave as he could. The small fire he had managed to build had nearly gone out several times within the hour. Each time the flames began to dwindle, he rushed to shield them with his body. It was pathetic. Billy Voss was as cold-blooded as they came, but he felt the cold here.

It was different from the icy comfort of the renovated Bakewell Ranch. Tendrils of a bitter freeze crawled through his veins as his breath quickened. He cursed himself for rushing into the wilderness unprepared and getting lost like a coward. His father would have been disappointed, to say the least, to have witnessed Billy's display of spinelessness.

He had been barely a man when he had been recruited for the army—shipped off to fight in a war he had wanted no part of—only to return to claim his birthright as the head of the Voss empire of immoral bribery and misappropriation. His family breathed fraud as fluently as others spoke a second language. They used pretty words to hide the fact that they were petty conmen.

When one business failed, the next rose up from the ashes and thrived until its inevitable demise. Keeping the same front for too long was sloppy. Staying in one place for more than three years was irresponsible. Constantly moving, constantly changing the way he operated, Billy Voss had outgrown his father's and his grandfather's accomplishments. Where they were content with false bookkeeping, tax evasion, and document fraud, Billy had taken his father's advice and built a dream out of it.

An unseen predator bayed at the rising sun. Billy ghosted his hand over the grip of his revolver and stiffened at the sound. His eyes scanned the trees as his hearing amplified to an almost animalistic level as though the hunter in him was responding to the one he could not perceive in that instant. He did not know what beasts lingered in the shadows, but he tamped down his fear and focused on steadying his erratic heartbeat. "Come on..." he breathed in a sound so quiet it was barely a whisper against the wind.

How many times had he dreamed of something similar? How many times had he looked down upon himself lying in wait to be caught unaware by some unknown enemy? Billy failed to keep track. The only difference between reality and the dreams was that he was not surrounded by a swirling spectrum of iridescent colors. No, this was real, and someone or something watched him from beyond his line of sight.

A branch snapped to his right, and Billy pulled the trigger on his revolver. The *crack* reverberated through the smattering of bare trees, mocking his fear and backing him up further against the stones behind him. An eerie silence hovered above the ground like the morning fog that dawdled in the phantom light of the rising sun. Normally, the sight before him and the quiet would have been tranquil.

But Billy did not have time to bask in the glow of serenity as Samuel "Cully" McCullough broke through the line of trees in front of his tragic little campsite. The bounty hunter's eyes darkened with hues of anger and... pity. Billy didn't want his pity. He didn't want anyone's pity.

Cully had seen the raw fear and madness in the face of Billy Voss. There was no doubt in his mind that the man who shivered before him was troubled beyond comprehension. Many times he had seen the side effects of a soul broken down by a lifetime of lies and regret. Voss was in way over his head, but the façade he had woven around himself refused to fracture so that common sense could seep through the cracks.

He brought his eyes up to the revolver that was leveled at his head and raised his hands in mock surrender, unwilling to end up with a bullet between the eyes because Billy Voss had an itchy trigger finger. Although it appeared like the once proud businessman from the eastern part of the country was at war with his thoughts, Cully could see the coward hidden behind the disheveled fancy clothing. "Easy now..." he said in the same voice he used when calming a horse.

"Don't come any closer," Voss warned.

"You ain't killed anybody yet. I know you're not that sort of man, Voss. And you know I could reach for my own pistol and fire off a shot long before you pulled the trigger on yours. So... why don't we talk this out?"

"Talk all you want, but I'm not going to jail. You seem so eager to make me see the error of my ways, but there are things about me that you don't understand, Mr.

McCullough," the man said like his words came from a distant place in his mind. His hand quaked profusely.

"I don't have to understand you to know that you don't deserve to die. Not unless that's how you want your story to end." Cully cautioned a slow, calculated step away from where he stood. "But I reckon that ain't how you imagined this gettin' settled. The sun is risin' on a beautiful day so far."

"Is this where you pretend to be sympathetic? Because I've been doing this for a long time, and I know a con when I smell one. And you reek of pretty speeches and smiles that don't reach your eyes. How many times do you rehearse these lines, Mr. McCullough?"

"Ain't gonna lie, I've used them a time or two. But I used them enough to know that they can defuse a situation before it gets too far out of control," he muttered sensibly. "Just because you've felt hollow inside for this long, don't mean there ain't nothin' human left inside ya."

"You don't know what you're talking about—"

"Been doin' my job for many years as well, sometimes I think too long. But I see the fright in your eyes just as easily as I can see the bags under them. Sleepless nights and memories that haunt your every wakin' hour ain't foreign to me, Voss. You can bet on that."

The other man snorted a short, half-amused huff of laughter, but his gun never lowered. There was the tight set of his jaw as he clenched his teeth against frosty air. Snow began to flutter softly toward the ground. It melted against the heat of Cully's shoulders and soaked into the fabric of his jacket.

Small puffs of smoke streamed continuously through his nostrils as he gulped past the cough that tickled his throat. He stared at Voss with an expression negated of all emotion, but he kept his voice steady. "Now, I'm gonna give you the same option I give everyone else who wants to call themselves my enemy. You can surrender, walk away, and go to a fair trial where you may one day be a free man. Or you can do what so many have foolishly done before you. Use that gun in your hand, attempt to kill me, and spend your last seconds on earth regrettin' your decision." Cully took another step forward and watched Voss's eyes widen.

"You wouldn't do that..."

"I would if you gave me no other choice. My work requires that I bring you to justice for the crimes you committed and the threats you made. But my nature and my instincts as an older brother demand that I hunt you down and make you pay for even considerin' hurtin' my family." The venom behind Cully's words was not lost in the gusts of wind that blew the powdery snow on the ground around his booted feet. With a motion that came with a speed that rivaled the blink of an eye, Cully had a revolver in his hand.

His long arms caused his gun to come up just inches from Voss's face. Panic forced the man to drop his gun as Cully bit the inside of his cheek to stifle the wince that came from witnessing someone handle a firearm so carelessly. Voss's hands came up in a show of surrender that was much like the one Cully had previously displayed. There was a moment that he allowed the crook to stew in his fear and reveled in the doubt in his eyes. "Please... don't kill me."

"I ain't gonna kill you, Voss. You ain't worth the tarnish that killin' you would cause on my soul." Cully lowered his gun and moved behind the still-juddering swindler. He pulled the length of rope from his belt and tied up his latest catch before hoisting Voss's fidgeting body onto the saddle of his horse. Cully whistled for Samson and mounted his back once he was within reach.

With one hand on the reins of Voss's horse and the other gripping Samson's, Cully led the mounts through the forest carefully. He made sure that they didn't stumble over the uneven ground or trip over each other. The man tied on the back of the horse sat in silence with his hands gripping the saddle horn with white knuckles and his lips pressed into a thin line. Cully took a deep breath in through his nose.

Billy Voss listened as Cully sighed. He squeezed his hands tighter against the leather that protruded from the saddle. No doubt the bounty hunter had picked up on his discomfort of riding horses and his lack of familiarity with the landscape. He assumed that Cully's short-lived hunt had probably been one of the fastest retrievals in his career. A fact that would have been embarrassing for Billy if he even cared.

"Ask," he offered. "I know you want to ask, to figure out if there's some semblance of hope for me. Lord, I can practically smell the heat coming off your overworked mind as you try to figure out if I'm simply *misunderstood*."

Although he could not see the thoughtful frown on Cully's face as he rode ahead, Billy had seen the expression on the man's face enough times in the short span of knowing him that it was simply expected. "Fine. Why do you do this? What motivates an obviously well-educated man with a military career to stoop so low?"

"You picked up on the military bit, huh? Anyway, the answer is the same reason *you* do everything. I do it for family, Mr. McCullough. To continue the legacy that my father and his father before him had built."

"So you turn to petty crime?"

"It was the family business." Voss's voice cracked with emotion as he whispered, "Haven't you ever wanted to make your father proud? To finally see something in his eyes other than tolerance or disappointment?"

It was Cully's turn to snort in bitter amusement. The events of the past few weeks most likely played out in his head along with images from his upbringing in Durango.

Billy watched Cully's head tilt to the side before he answered.

"My father died before he could see me become a man. I know what you mean though. Benjamin McCullough was a shinin' light in this community, and it was hard some days to be his son. Heck, even to this day I find myself strugglin' to come out from behind his shadow. But he tried his best to make sure I had a good head on my shoulders, and he provided for his family. You didn't have to end up like your father."

"You wouldn't say that if you met the man. Guess it's no excuse for my actions. Judgment was bound to come in one form or the other. Destiny always has a way of showing up when we least expect it to."

"You know what, Voss? In another life—if you weren't a criminal, and I wasn't a bounty hunter—I would have offered to buy you a drink down at the saloon."

For the second time since his arrest, Billy found himself not only amused but also confessing his life's story to Samuel McCullough. It was a shock to both men as he finally revealed the history that had been a complete secret until that moment.

Chapter 11

Cully panted strained breaths as the wetness of his clothing began to weigh down his movements in the saddle. His muscles protested against the added bulk. An irritable grunt from over his shoulder implied that Voss felt the same. The weather was ugly and cold, so both riders were eager to get indoors. Probably the only time Billy Voss would willingly walk into a sheriff's office without coercion.

Winters in Colorado were unforgiving and brutal to those who were not accustomed to the changes of seasons. Despite how often he complained about the cold, one of Cully's favorite things about the region was the December rain that he watched through the window of his home.

Cully once again unfolded himself out of the saddle and stretched above his head with a noisy groan as his back cracked obscenely. The streets were nearly empty as folks waited out the cold with their loved one's indoors. Part of Cully was annoyed that he had missed his supper just to chase yet another amateur coward.

He eased the horses to the livery stables in town so that they would be tended to and shielded from the harsh winds. Cully handed Samson and the other horse off to the boys at the stables. The sky was filled with dark clouds as the snow continued to fall, battling against the slight rays of sunlight that tried to peek through. He helped Voss off the back of his horse and escorted him into Sheriff Lassiter's office.

He walked the man into the building with a hand firmly wrapped around his forearm, guiding him along the way, as well as making sure that Voss didn't attempt another escape. At first, Sheriff Lassiter was nowhere to be found after Cully closed the door behind them and thanked the heavens that the heat had finally been fixed.

"Hey, Jake!" Cully called. After the sheriff hobbled his way across the room, he stopped just short of the criminal in Cully's custody. "I need you to book Billy Voss and get him settled into a cell. He won't fight you. Already got a confession out of him on the way back."

Sheriff Lassiter looked as though he wanted to protest against Cully's casual demeanor toward the threats Voss had been tossing around Durango. He knew most people would take it personally, even he had at one point. But after seeing the way Voss had shrunken under the intimidation he had applied in kind, Cully didn't believe that the man's actions were of any threat on people's lives. No matter how coldhearted his words had seemed, there was only damage done to personal property and not the individual themselves.

Property could be rebuilt and repurchased, but there was no price that could be paid for the lost life of another human. It was a value Cully had learned the day his parents had died. There had been nothing he was unwilling to sacrifice in their stead. However, as Voss had mentioned, destiny always had a way of showing up when you least expected.

"Jake..."

"All right, I'll take him and lock him up. Don't know how you get them to surrender the way you do, but I hope you decide to show a few of us one of these days. I'm gettin' too old to be chasin' down scoundrels left and right. I ain't cut out for this the way I used to be," the sheriff said as he nodded to Cully.

"Any word from your connections?"

"Pinkertons sent word from back east. They have some evidence that will help with the trial. Left it on the desk, thought you might want to a have a look at it," Sheriff Lassiter informed him as he replaced Cully's grip on Voss's arm with his own. Cully watched them disappear near the back of the building before he walked over to the desk and picked up the file that was haphazardly tossed on top.

He flipped through the first few pages of information that Voss had already confessed on their ride into town. Some useless drivel from public records, nothing incriminating for Billy Voss specifically until he had reached the age of fifteen. The earlier evidence had been the result of William Voss Sr., Billy's father who had been suspected on several accounts of embezzlement and fraud.

The list of alleged crimes committed by William Voss Sr. filled the majority of the file. When Cully came across the evidence against Billy Voss, there was no denying the connections between the crimes. He had nearly followed perfectly in his father's footsteps until the first arson in Pennsylvania that, of course, could not be proven.

Cully scrubbed a hand down the stubble on his cheek and continued reading through the file.

Several scam companies and gimmicky trades carried out under Billy Voss's name were scattered all throughout the states along the eastern coast. He moved from one town to the next each time his antics were called out.

That was, until he eventually made his way to Chicago, where he was accused of coercion and embezzlement. Cully thought of the "book of debts" that Voss had tucked in his pocket during his arrest. The one now in Cully's possession.

It wasn't until Billy Voss had supplied fraudulent ownership documents for several plots of land belonging to a small town in the Midwest that the Pinkertons gained an interest in the Voss family business.

They had put together quite a substantial file, but it hadn't been enough to warrant an arrest or justify a bounty. Therefore, the detectives investigating the case had been forced to stay their hand, even after Voss left the state. With no evidence and a missing suspect in over two hundred open cases of embezzlement, the investigation had gone cold until Sheriff Lassiter sent his inquiry after Voss moved into the Bakewell Ranch.

The amounts of land that had been acquired through shady deals were astonishing. Cully could barely believe how much Billy Voss was actually worth—if not in sheer numbers then in property value. If he had made it far enough without falling into one of Cully's traps, Voss *could* have bought half of Durango as he had claimed. There was an unsettling amount of underestimation where Voss was concerned.

An idea struck him just as Sheriff Lassiter returned to the main office. "Do you think we can offer Voss a deal?"

"What are you gettin' at, Cully?"

"Perhaps if we offer Voss an opportunity to turn his father and grandfather in to the authorities, they'll be more lenient toward him at trial—at least for the embezzlement. There ain't no prettyin' up the arson, but…"

"Wait one darn minute," the sheriff interrupted. "You mean to tell me, on the little ride down here from where he was hidin', you had a change of heart big enough to offer him a deal? He threatened Doris, Cully. You were forced to kill three outlaws so that they didn't harm your family. You sure you want to do that?"

"Doris would preach forgiveness in this situation until both of us were bleedin' out our ears, and you know it. Voss told me he ain't really spent a dime of the money he got runnin' his bogus deals. He ain't a materialistic person, despite how greedy he seems for power."

"What do you suggest?"

"He pays off a hefty fine as well as payin' for the damages done to the properties he destroyed. Voss should also have to return ownership to all the land he claimed usin' illegal methods of attainment. Turn in his father and grandfather to stop the embezzlement once and for all. In return, he gets on the next train out of Durango, goes back east, and acquires a reduced punishment for his cooperation."

It sounded logical to his ears, so Cully thought that was the best he could do for a troubled soldier who had been roped into his family's manipulations. The end results were out of his hands, but he hoped his recommendation would serve as a lesson learned that no good could come of taking advantage of others. Cully ran a hand through the hair at the nape of his neck that slightly curled over the collar of his jacket, his fingers momentarily snagging on a few knots.

The smell of gunpowder and leather danced across his senses and mingled with the humid smell of the sheriff's office. He wanted a bath nearly as much as he wanted the matter with Billy Voss settled so he could go home. Cully waited for Sheriff Lassiter to send word to the Pinkertons and communicate his offer to the state marshal. Due to the Voss family crimes expanding over several states, the matter was under federal jurisdiction. Which meant there was no bounty or reward for the arrest and nothing else he could do for the case.

It amazed Cully how a simple favor for a friend could turn into an adventure that caused him to ponder his choices in life.

"You know, you're the only one lookin' past what others would have assumed they knew how to handle. You took it that one step further where you almost became somebody else. It's like you set your emotions and opinions aside and looked at things from an entirely different perspective. I respect that. Your father would have been proud of you today. Benjamin McCullough was a great man, and so are you. You're so much like him, it's almost eerie sometimes."

"My parents were wonderful people who were loyal to their community and to the church. What happened to them and everyone else that was lost that day was tragic. It left me with a hole in my chest that can never be mended," Cully admitted. "But it also gave me a purpose and a headstrong sister to look after. So I don't need to feel their pride. It's enough to know that they are at peace."

The sharp slap on his shoulder and the wet gaze of Sheriff Lassiter was all he needed to know that he had made the correct decision to bring Voss in alive. If he had simply gunned down the lawbreaker, he would have missed several opportunities to have some much-needed conversations.

Chapter 12

For a moment, the sound of knocking on the hotel room door sounded like gunshots. Doris jerked awake, a pillow crease along her neck, and blinked open her sleep-dazed eyes. She pulled on the robe she had packed in her bag and went to peek through a small crack she opened in the door.

Her heart quickened at the sight of her brother as she flung herself into his arms.

His deep, raspy chuckle made her realize just how much she had worried for his safety, as the tears she had withheld began to fall. Cully pulled Doris into a warm embrace as he whispered words of comfort in her ear. He hadn't had to comfort her like this since they were kids, but she was grateful for the support.

"Sorry I didn't come back right away. I should have at least sent word that I was all right," he said sheepishly. "There were just a lot of loose ends that needed to be tied up before I could relax some. Don't you cry, Doris Ann."

Doris pulled away and checked the small clock that ticked by the hours. It was almost noon, but she couldn't care less. She tugged Cully into the room by the sleeve of his jacket and led him over to a chair near the window. He looked up at her with a furrowed brow as she stood over him with her arms crossed over her middle. The serious expression she wore on her face gave him a bit of worry, she could tell.

"Tell me I placed my faith in the right man, Sam."

"What are you gettin' at?"

Her tongue darted out briefly to wet her dry lips as she rocked on her heels. "You didn't… ugh, you let him live, didn't you? Please, tell me you didn't do anything foolish."

"Billy Voss is alive. Once I heard the whole story, I couldn't let him take the full blame. So I got him a deal. He wasn't like the men I was used to huntin' down. He ain't a killer, just a man who had been raised to abuse power."

Doris released a breath she hadn't realized she'd been holding. Her knees buckled slightly, and she sat in the chair across from Cully. Relief and understanding finally allowed her to meet his questioning gaze. "Guess all my talk of forgiveness, mercy, and salvation finally got through that stubbornness."

The creaking of the floorboards meant their conversation had awakened Ethan. His hair stuck out in too many directions. His half-shut eyes, and the way he almost collapsed against Doris as he wrapped his arms around her, was a testament to how exhausted he was. She snickered a little and turned to see him resting his forehead against her shoulder. The only words that came out of his sleep-dry mouth was a croaked, "Mornin'," which caused both the McCullough siblings to giggle.

"Nice work with that shotgun, Ethan." Cully wasn't known for complimenting his brother-in-law so openly, mostly because there had always been a part of him that thought no man was good enough for his little sister. But he had always been polite, if not stern, with the younger man.

There was no bad blood between them, and Cully respected Ethan's sense of responsibility. Doris was just glad that her brother hadn't shot her husband the day he found out they were getting married.

"Thank you, Cully. Although, I must say that I had hoped there wouldn't have been a need to use it," Ethan replied.

Doris placed a chaste kiss against her husband's cheek before she offered her seat to him. Once the two most important men in her life were settled, she looked between them before finally addressing Cully once again. "Tell us about what happened, Sam."

"Well, after Voss took off into the woods, it wasn't hard to track him down. He didn't seem to know where he was goin' or what kind of animals may have been out there lookin' for somethin' to hunt. Nearly got spotted by a few coyotes, but luckily he had a little fire goin' to keep them away through the darker hours. Found him once the sun started to rise..."

Doris reached over and placed a hand on her brother's. She didn't think Cully had been aware that he had gripped his hands into fists so tight his knuckles cracked. Once he took a deep breath, some of her worry faded.

"He was a mess. Looked like he was fightin' with his own mind, mumblin' to himself about things I couldn't understand, to be honest. As much as I hated to admit it, Billy Voss looked like I did whenever the memories came hauntin' my dreams. You don't walk away from a life like mine without scars. But in those few seconds, I saw the tiredness take hold."

"Tiredness?" Ethan asked.

"It's soul deep. Not somethin' that comes from exhaustion of the mind or the body but from your spirit. It comes when those urges to give in take hold of you. He wasn't as strong as I was, so I knew all I had to do was get him talkin', and he would surrender. But it was hard to look past the ire that I felt toward him for threatenin' my family and this town. Luckily my sympathy was sturdier."

Doris squeezed Cully's hands in her own and poured her emotions into her eyes, praying that he saw just how much he meant to her. She didn't like how defeated his words sounded. "What else happened, Sam?"

"He had a gun pointed at me, but I got him to calm down just by lettin' him talk. Realized that he had been broken under the pressure that his father put on him, but his time in the war had done its fair share of damage. All of that together and I think he just didn't like takin' orders anymore. This was his way of takin' back the control he felt he had been deprived."

There was more to what Cully had to say. And Doris thought she should let him open up when he wanted to instead of pressuring him to talk. The three of them had gone through the motions of washing up, eating breakfast, and changing into a fresh set of clothes before the conversation continued.

"He didn't put up a fight when I arrested him. But I took a moment to let him fear me. And I enjoyed it so much that I understood that it was somethin' I had done for years. Outlaws fear the day that I'm on their trail, and it feels powerful. Even though I went about it differently and for a bunch of reasons, there ain't much of a variance between me and Billy Voss, from what I can tell."

Doris slammed her hand flat on the table, causing Ethan and Cully to stare at her with wide eyes. "That's enough! You've done a lot of good, Sam. And I won't let you talk down on yourself in my presence."

Ethan shook his head. "I agree with her, Cully. No one has rescued as many people as you have. No one has sacrificed as much as you have, and they definitely haven't changed as many people's lives as you. Now, I know you don't see yourself as a hero of any sort, but that doesn't mean that you're like Billy."

"No, you don't understand. I've killed. There's blood on my hands that can't be washed away, no matter how hard I try. I've caused damage that I can't even begin to repair. While I've never left a man behind willingly or betrayed a trust, I've profited off of people's problems over the years. I'm ashamed at times by how often I've allowed myself to play God."

"Sam, you told me before that you didn't need my support or my approval. You said that you only needed me to understand that what you were doing was important. Now that I've seen the danger this life has to offer, I do understand. Those men were heavily armed and firing their guns into our house. They burned down our barn and set fire to Denis Seeley's homestead. If it weren't for you, things could have been so much worse." Doris reached around the back of her neck and unclasped her necklace.

From her fingers dangled a thin chain with a small silver cross that had once belonged to their mother. Doris pressed a kiss to the cross and placed it in the callused palm of Cully's hand. He stared at it as though he waited for the metal to heat up and burn through his skin.

"I'm not saying that you've always done the right thing, Sam. Or that your actions don't have consequences. But you are a righteous man with good intentions. The people you've helped know this and are forever grateful."

Doris and Ethan watched Cully brush the pad of his thumb across the smooth silvery surface of the charm before he curled his long fingers around it.

"Thank you," he said thickly, his twang colored every word. Ethan placed his hand on Cully's shoulder, understanding just how important the necklace had been to Doris. She met her husband's gaze and silently thanked him for being her anchor as she healed from a damaged past.

Now that he offered her brother the same support, Doris was sure she couldn't have loved him more than she did just then. She pretended to not notice the way the nerve in Cully's jaw ticked as he clenched his teeth as he fought back a few sniffles. He was a proud man after all.

A warm smile appeared on Doris's face. "Everyone will need time to recover from all of this. Stay home for a while, Sam. Help rebuild. God and those around you will forgive your actions over the years, but it's your own forgiveness that matters most. Without it, you'll never be able to move on."

Chapter 13

Cully walked to the area where people took their water breaks as they assisted with the restoration of Denis Seeley's property. Most of the barn had been rebuilt since Cully's last visit. He spotted Denis kneeling beside a large fire in an adjacent field where the debris burned.

"Jake told me that you got Billy Voss a deal with the Marshal," Denis said accusingly but without malice. "He would have hurt a lot of people if you hadn't arrested him."

He knew not everyone would be happy about his decision where Voss was concerned. But Cully didn't believe that justice would have been served if he had chosen a different outcome. Even so, what's done is done. He couldn't change it any more than he had control over the weather, which was surprisingly pleasant after several days of nonstop snow.

"He's payin' for what he did, don't you worry, sir. You and everybody else he took advantage of will be paid a hefty sum for the trouble he caused as well as reimbursement for the renewal of all the damaged property. Whoever's land he obtained usin' illegal means will get it back without a problem."

Cully watched some frustration bleed out of Denis's posture. It was replaced with an overwhelming amount of fatigue that caused the older gentleman to hunch his shoulders. Cully was well aware that the people of Durango had been collectively holding their breath, waiting for Cully to right the wrongs of Billy Voss. After everything had been settled and his talk with Doris and Ethan, Cully had made his rounds through town and surrounding area, making sure to stop in to speak with the folks most affected by the threats and arson.

He had even paid a visit to the Montoya Ranch to check on Ruby and Felix after their run-in with Voss and his gang. Everyone seemed to be slowly moving forward with each day—a sign that better days were soon to come for everybody.

"I ain't gonna lie, Denis. There were several times when I didn't believe you or I felt the urge to walk away from an impossible situation. But family goes beyond blood, and I've known you since I was a child, so I had to set this right."

"I see you as family too, Cully. And I'm glad you're honest with me. I didn't think this could end in a way that didn't involve me and Alice movin' out of Durango, but I'm happy we get to stay. Can't think of a better place to call home." Denis moved closer and hugged Cully with a few pats on the back. Cully returned the gesture and left Denis to his thoughts.

He walked over to Alice Seeley who was busying herself with painting the outside of the barn, along with a few of the ranch hands. The paint on her forehead made Cully wonder if there was ever a time in her life that Alice hadn't been smeared with some sort of mess.

Even as a little girl, she had trailed after him and a few of the other boys, eager to join in their games of mischief, but always covered in dirt or mud, with leaves and twigs tangled in her hair.

He smiled fondly at one of the happy memories of his childhood, feeling the tension slowly drain from his muscles. Happiness was a rarity for him of late, so he wanted to savor each moment. Cully didn't point out the smudge on her face and simply continued to smile. Alice finally caught sight of him as she tripped over the container of paint on the ground.

Cully's reflexes kicked in, and he caught Alice just above her elbow to keep her from falling over. Her cheeks turned a charming shade of pink before she set down her brush and wiped her hands against her dress. He handed her his handkerchief like before and watched her fuss over her appearance.

"Thank you, for everything. It's been a little rough picking up the pieces and putting things back together."

"How are things, Alice? We ain't talked in a while."

"For all the love of the Lord above, Mr. McCullough," Alice laughed in frustration.

His expression was one of shock and confusion.

"Now I know why the ladies of this town are so fond of you. Just riding into Durango to save the day, and then you act calm and mysterious, all while you blush from here to heaven. It should be a crime, you batting those pretty eyes..."

"My eyes?" he croaked, unsure and self-conscious beyond belief. Cully felt heat crawl up his neck and settle on his face. Alice had never been one to withhold the truth of her words, even if she was a little shy, but it still caught him off guard with how comfortably she had just spoken to him. The cold against his skin was now a welcome relief from his current state of embarrassment.

"Mm-hmm. Like sunlight shining off a glass of whiskey or a jar of warm honey. No doubt you're a wonderful poker player, but those eyes give away a lot more than you think. My prayers go out to the woman who steals your heart, Mr. McCullough. She might not take too kindly to the stares that come your way." Alice turned back to her painting but stayed within a distance that allowed comfortable conversation.

"Well, I, uh…" he stumbled. "You never answered my question. How are you, Alice? I know it's been a lot of hard work, and I can tell you've been workin' yourself to the bone."

"I'm not going to lie and say it's been easy. But I get by."

"That ain't an answer, Alice. It's a deflection."

Alice's laughter chimed out in a bold, natural flow of sound that caused everyone within hearing distance to smile.

He kicked a rock with his boot, trying to hide the fact that he enjoyed making the people in his life happy. It was an effort to keep his reputation of being calm and mysterious as Alice had said.

"You're the master of deflection, Mr. McCullough."

"Please, call me Cully. We've known each other for years, and I don't call you *Miss Seeley*." He didn't want to be so formal with someone he had known his entire life.

"If you insist, *Cully*," she said cheekily. "I'm not feeling well, and my back is killing me. I'd do just about anything for a foot rub or a warm bed to sleep in, but I'm not doing any better or worse than anyone else here. Not really one to complain. How's that for honesty?"

"Better," he replied stubbornly. Earning him another one of her cheerful laughs. Cully looked over to see a young man with the same look on his face that Ethan had worn around Doris during their courtship. "I can see Alex is sweet on you."

"Reminds me of my previous fiancé, but he's a friendly guy. It's a shame that my heart has always belonged to someone else—someone who always fails to see my heart on my sleeve whenever they're around. Tragic love and all that..."

The wistful note in her voice and pleading gaze caused Cully's head to drop down to his boots, pretending to be lost in thought. He couldn't find the strength to look at Alice or ask the questions he dare not speak. Cully settled for the two words he said most often, "I'm sorry."

"Don't be. I'm not. There's someone special out there for you, Cully. Just try to be patient. You've got a mighty large family already. The rest will fall into place. Have faith."

Chapter 14

Cully sat in his favorite chair and put his feet up on the small stool that allowed him to stretch his long legs. After shedding his worn-out clothes, bathing, shaving, and even trimming his hair, he felt some stress from the last few weeks disappear. Sleeping in the barn and camping out on Denis Seeley's land had been worth the trouble, though.

He wouldn't have been able to leave his friends and family unprotected during Voss's rampage.

A lot of folks who didn't spend their time on the road wouldn't understand the constant ache in Cully's bones, the times he woke up and his mouth tasted like he had spent the night licking the inside of his own boot, or the days he missed seeing other people so much he felt starved.

Life was bleak when all he had to eat for weeks or months was campfire stew, dry biscuits, and jerky so tough he may as well gnaw the leather of his belt. Cully wouldn't wish his own cooking on his worst enemy.

But he knew sooner rather than later, he would accept another contract and be pulled away from Durango and the comfort of his home once again. As much as he would have hated to admit it a few months back, Cully felt a change within himself. Maybe there was some validity in Doris's words.

For so long he wondered whether he was beyond redemption or if he was taking that seemingly inevitable fall to the other side of the line of right and wrong. The other side that would no longer set him apart from the outlaws he hunted.

Cully closed his eyes and toyed with the small cross that fell between the open buttons at the neck of his shirt. It was warm from his skin, and although it was smaller than the tip of his finger, there was a weight to the chain. It held every expectation that Doris had of him as well as the constant reminder of their parents and what they had lost.

Not much in the world could make Samuel McCullough feel weak, but each time his memory took him back down that dark road, he felt the impossibly strong urge to just run again. But Cully knew if he ran away, abandoning everything he built and all the people he had grown to care for, he would never come back. Ever.

So he settled for humoring the idea that there was more to himself than what he always thought. There were two sides to him: Cully, the famous bounty hunter, and then Samuel, the man who yearned for an ordinary life. But as long as there was evil in the west, he wouldn't allow himself to settle down any more than he already had.

He huffed out an irritable sigh.

Even when he forced himself to relax, his mind was back on the road. The quietness that swept through the house made him consider finding himself a dog. Samson was a great horse, but he wasn't allowed inside the house, no matter how amusing of a sight that would have been. There were plenty of mangy pups wandering around out there that needed a home.

And heck, Cully wanted something to come home to.

Especially after he pooled together his funds to start building his own ranch. All the recent talk about forgiveness and his thoughts on having a normal life was... different.

His dreams and aspirations seemed within reach, finally, after all the years of doubt and discouragement.

A sharp knock on the door had him rolling his eyes and shuffling to his feet. Out of habit, he reached for his firearm but quickly set it aside when he saw who was on his porch. As soon as his hand turned the doorknob, Doris pushed her way inside. There was a ray of light that caused her to glow.

She looked like an angel with her barely there freckles and shining smile. The snow that fluttered around her seemed to dance happily as Cully closed the door to keep the warmth inside. Doris tugged the scarf from around her neck and hung it up along with her coat.

The bottom of her dress was a bit wet from the ground, and she rubbed her hands together to get some warmth back into her fingers. Still, her infectious smile brightened the dreary interior of his home as he brushed the snow out of her hair. "I did it, Sam!"

"Did what, Doris Ann?"

"I'll be teaching at the schoolhouse once the kids are back in class and the more pleasant weather returns," Doris said with a little happy dance. Her nose was a bit red from the cold, but she was happier than he'd seen in a long time. Cully knew how much she loved children and couldn't wait until the day Doris became a mother.

"You'll be wonderful. You got them natural instincts."

"Do you think they'll like me, Sam? I mean... I have never been a teacher before, but I've done a lot of work with the church and the families there. I'm so worried I'll mess this up now that I've got the opportunity."

Cully brushed aside her uncertainties and nodded his head. He moved Doris into the kitchen and prepared a pot of coffee for himself but kept enough hot water to make her a cup of tea.

She accepted the oversized mug and chuckled.

An intriguing thought entered his mind... "How'd you get here on your own, Doris Ann?" When her cheeks grew flushed, he just knew her answer would surprise him. But he hadn't been prepared in the least.

"I stole Ethan's horse."

Cully sputtered at her words. He looked at Doris with a confusing expression of shock and hilarity all at once. No, not his darling, innocent, caring, saintly little sister...

Cully couldn't help the laughter that erupted from his chest at the mental image of Doris rustling up her skirts to pilfer her husband's horse, just to tell her older brother some good news.

He couldn't believe it. Even now, Doris was an image of propriety and elegance. "You did not!"

"What was I supposed to do? Wait?"

"Patience is a virtue," he scolded half-heartedly. "Who would have thought that you were capable of such a thing? I'm surprised at you. Since when are you so rebellious?"

"It only happens when you're in town," Doris grumbled around her cup of tea. "You're a bad influence, Sam."

"Fine. Go ahead and blame me."

"Gladly."

And just like that, Cully laughed with uninhibited delight once more. The honesty of his mirth summoned a similar response in Doris. Within seconds, she collapsed into a fit of giggles and was forced to wipe tears from her eyes. "Guess it does seem sort of silly now that I think about it."

"Just a little." He sent her a wink.

"I was just so excited when they accepted me, and I guess... I guess I just wanted to make you proud. You always said I shouldn't limit myself to just being somebody's wife."

"And I still believe it. I am very proud of the woman you've become over the years, Doris Ann. I know my big brother instincts can be overbearing and don't allow me to see you as anything other than my little sister, but I'm proud of you no matter what. There ain't no hope in me changin', though."

"I wouldn't want you to change, Sam."

They sipped their steaming beverages and watched through the window in the kitchen as a light snow continued to fall beyond the frosted glass.

Doris looked around his home with a skeptical eye and a carefully arched brow.

"What?" he asked self-consciously.

"It's a bit empty, isn't it? I know you're gone a lot, but how about some flowers or..."

"A wife?" Cully returned her expression with a high brow and a cunning smirk of his own. "Still keen on playin' matchmaker, Doris Ann?"

"Well…" and there it was, that all-telling blush again. "I don't think I'll stop until I see you at the marriage altar with my own eyes. This place could use a little womanly touch, don't you think? Maybe… Alice? Or… or maybe the woman who saved your life when you were away? What was her name? Maria!"

Cully lifted his hand to cut off her train of thought, which was dangerous, involved friends, and clearly included him in some form of domestic bliss he couldn't even fathom. "Sometimes I think you forget I'm your brother, and that everythin' you know about plottin' and schemin', you learned from the best. And that would be me, in case you forgot. Now, why don't we ride to Durango and start puttin' this town back together?"

She snorted in defeat. "Fine. I won't bring it back up again—at least not today, anyway. You're right, of course. I shouldn't pry into your personal life. It's rude, and I apologize, Sam. I just want you to be happy. You win. This time."

As much as her words sounded genuine, Cully knew her better than to believe anything she said with that smile creeping across her lips. Nope, he wasn't about to fall for any of her tricks. He cleared his throat and dislodged that pleased expression off her face. "I'm sure you'll find a way to weasel it back into the conversation at some point. You never really were one for subtly where I was concerned. Just… don't do it around other people, all right? Last thing I need is for folks to realize that I'm bad at talkin' to women for more than five minutes."

Doris threw her head back in laughter. "Anybody who has ever seen you talkin' to a woman knows that you act like a child on Christmas morning. All flustered, stumbling over your words, and happy just for the attention."

"I don't like the attention."

"That red on your cheeks calls you a liar, Sam."

Cully looked down timidly. "What happened to that renowned sense of propriety of yours?"

"Like I said, it only happens when you're here. You really are a bad influence," she replied with a smile so impishly wicked that it belied her angelic look.

Rascal, Cully thought.

Epilogue

Sweat beaded on Cully's forehead and dripped into his eyes, causing them to burn. He pushed his hat higher and brushed the sweat away with the back of his glove as he worked alongside the good people of Durango. After Doris and Ethan's barn had been rebuilt, he put his efforts toward finishing the Seeley barn until moving on to the restoration of the main house. The first level had been completely remodeled with enough room for Alice to have her own space.

Cully worked on finishing the roof with Ethan as some others painted and put the final touches on the interior of the house. It wouldn't be the same as it had been before, but Denis was happy with the changes. Everyone was eager to move on from the damage done by Billy Voss.

He looked over to Ethan to see him in the same sweat-drenched state that Cully was in. They shared a brief chuckle before Ethan grew serious. "I want you to know that I can keep her safe, Cully. There are times that I feel as though you don't completely trust me with Doris's safety."

"I trust you, Ethan. But Doris and I have been through a lot together, so it's only natural that I worry for her well-being. She's a strong, intelligent woman who knows her own mind. And if she chose you, there has to be a good enough reason," Cully explained. "She loves you and you're family.

That's all that matters. You handled yourself well against Voss's men, and I'm proud of you for takin' that necessary step. I trust you."

"You don't know what a relief it is to hear you say that, Cully. I've been fighting for even an inch of your approval for so long—even well before Doris and I got married—that I can barely remember a time that I didn't look up to you. You're not an easy man to approach, but it's hard not to admire you."

Cully reached over and patted Ethan on the shoulder. It was a much-needed conversation they should have had long ago, but that McCullough stubbornness hadn't allowed it to happen. To be honest, Cully had dodged Ethan to avoid having a chat with the younger man. But with change came acceptance, and now he accepted Ethan like a brother.

"Let's get this finished up so we can go pester the others," Cully offered. He looked over to the fence line where a familiar figure walked through the pasture. Mateo Rodriguez stood several yards away from the barn. He looked healthy. His hair was cut short into a military style. He had shaven, and.... well, he looked civilized once again. Cully waved him over, but Mateo hesitated and shook his head.

Catching the hint, he climbed down the ladder and walked calmly over to his old friend. A man he had fought beside and nearly died protecting. A man who had saved his life too many times to count and still found a way to make it seem like he owed Cully a favor. "Mateo."

"Señor McCullough. It has been a while, amigo."

"That it has. I was glad to hear Maria is all right and your madre is in good health," Cully said, trying hard not to think of the awkward conversation he had shared with Doris a few days back. "What brings you to Durango?"

"I wanted to tell you in person that I finally found my son. His name is Emanuel. He is no more than four years old, but he already has my charms. I am staying in town for a while..."

"What is it, Mateo?" Cully asked, sensing a bit of worry.

"His mother was sick when I found her. She was able to say goodbye, but eventually she succumbed to her sickness. I brought him here to see if you knew anyone who could care for him until I return." Mateo's eyes avoided Cully's gaze like the plague. "There are still dangerous men after me, señor. Men like the one who took Maria. I would never forgive myself if anything happened to my child."

Cully looked up to the roof where Ethan hammered away at a particularly difficult nail. Before he realized exactly what he was doing, he led Mateo into Denis Seeley's newly built house and tapped on Doris's shoulder. She looked up at him with a frown until she noticed that he was not alone.

"Hello," she breathed as she cleaned her hands off on her apron before offering one to the man at her brother's side and smiled. "My name is Doris Hawes. I'm Cully's sister."

"Mateo Rodriguez. It is a pleasure to meet you, Señora Hawes. I am a friend of your brother's."

"I've heard so much about you," Doris stated as she looked at Cully questioningly.

He swallowed nervously but took a leap of faith. "Mateo is only in Durango for a short while, but he brought his son with him. He needs to leave on important business, but he can't take Emanuel with him. I was hoping..."

"How long?" she asked without hesitation.

Mateo answered, "I am not sure, but I hope three months at the very most. With occasional visits whenever I am in town. I do not want my son to not know me as his father."

"We can take him in. I'm sure Ethan wouldn't mind at all."

Cully exhaled a sigh of relief. "Thank you, Doris."

He then led Mateo back outside where the other man threw his arms around Cully and hugged him in a sign of affection he had never seen from Mateo. It only lasted for a few moments, but Cully knew he had done the right thing by offering Emanuel a safe place with his sister while Mateo dealt with his problems.

Even so, he pinned his friend with a harsh look. "I don't want to end up huntin' you down, Mateo. But I will if your *business* becomes mine. Got it? No need to go breakin' Maria's heart over somethin' foolish."

"I will not betray your trust, señor. There is no way I could ever repay you for your kindness."

Cully thought on that for a while. "Why don't you start by picking up a hammer and helpin' me out on the roof? That way you can get to know the man who will be lookin' after Emanuel while you're off takin' care of things."

"Of course."

It was a smooth day after that.

No one fell through floorboards, no one hammered their fingers, and no one spilled paint where it wasn't meant to be—other than all over Alice Seeley, of course. Alice's clumsiness had somehow unintentionally caught the eye of Mateo while he helped out on the roof.

Cully leaned forward and whopped his friend on the head, forcing him to focus on the task at hand. It was no one's business that Cully hid a slight smile of amusement, especially after he noticed how flustered both Mateo and Alice had been after he caught them making eyes at each other.

All in all, it turned out to be a good day. The house was finished and everyone settled down for a big dinner courtesy of Denis Seeley's home cooking.

Cully was surrounded by happiness and a strong sense of community. The love of those around him filled him with great joy and contentment. He watched with a smile tugging at the corner of his mouth as people danced, joked, and carried on without a care in the world. The sounds slowly faded into the background, and Cully allowed himself to be swept up by the atmosphere.

Doris would finally get her chance to care for a child. Mateo was safe and trying to right his wrongs. Ethan had thoroughly earned Cully's trust. Denis and Alice Seeley had their home back. All was right with the world.

This, this was what it was all about. Each dopey grin and obnoxious bout of laughter made every ounce of Cully's pain worth it. And then he was certain that he was on the path that God had chosen for him.

The End

Could I get you to consider leaving a review on Amazon? It would be appreciated.

More westerns are in the works.

34466420R10073